# COUNTRIES OF THE WORLD

# Algeria

CONTRA COSTA COUNTY LIBRARY

**Gareth Stevens Publishing**
A WORLD ALMANAC EDUCATION GROUP COMPANY

**About the Author:** William Mark Habeeb is a writer and foreign affairs consultant who has traveled widely throughout North Africa and the Middle East. He holds a Ph.D. in international politics from the Johns Hopkins University.

Written by
**WILLIAM MARK HABEEB**

Edited by
**PATRICIA NG
LYNELLE SEOW**

Edited in the U.S. by
**ERIK GOPEL
ALAN WACHTEL**

Designed by
**BENSON TAN**

Picture research by
**THOMAS KHOO
JOSHUA ANG**

First published in North America in 2005 by
**Gareth Stevens Publishing**
A World Almanac Education Group Company
330 West Olive Street, Suite 100
Milwaukee, Wisconsin 53212 USA

Please visit our web site at
www.garethstevens.com
For a free color catalog describing
Gareth Stevens Publishing's list of high-quality
books and multimedia programs, call
1-800-542-2595 (USA) or 1-800-387-3178 (Canada)
Gareth Stevens Publishing's fax: (414) 332-3567.

© **MARSHALL CAVENDISH INTERNATIONAL (ASIA) PRIVATE LIMITED 2004**
Originated and designed by
Times Editions Marshall Cavendish
An imprint of Marshall Cavendish International (Asia) Pte Ltd
A member of Times Publishing Limited
Times Centre, 1 New Industrial Road
Singapore 536196
http://www.timesone.com.sg/te

**Library of Congress Cataloging-in-Publication Data**
Habeeb, William Mark.
Algeria / by William Mark Habeeb.
p. cm. — (Countries of the world)
Includes bibliographic references and index.
ISBN 0-8368-3114-4 (lib. bdg.)
1. Algeria—Juvenile literature.
I. Title. II. Countries of the world (Milwaukee, Wis.)
DT275.H33 2004
965—dc22                2004048124

Printed in Singapore

1 2 3 4 5 6 7 8 9 08 07 06 05 04

# Contents

# AN OVERVIEW OF ALGERIA

Located in the northwestern region of Africa, Algeria is the tenth largest country in the world and the second largest country in Africa. A large part of Algeria is covered by the Sahara Desert, which is uninhabited except for a few small, isolated communities.

Many foreign influences are visible throughout Algeria, from the country's street signs to its music to its architecture. In the seventh century, the Arabs brought Islam into the country, and many Algerians converted to Islam. In the nineteenth century, Algeria was invaded by the French, who brought their culture and language into Algeria. Today, many Algerians speak French in addition to Arabic, the country's official language.

*Opposite:* **Nomads who live in the Algerian Sahara Desert have adapted to the harsh desert conditions. This nomad has wrapped his face to prevent sand from entering his nose and mouth.**

*Below:* **Algiers is the capital of Algeria. It is both the country's largest city and its political center.**

## THE FLAG OF ALGERIA

**The Algerian flag features two vertical columns of green and white, with a red crescent moon and a star at the center. Green is the traditional color of Islam. White signifies purity, and red stands for liberty. The crescent moon is an important symbol in the Middle East. It was adopted by the Ottoman Turks as a symbol of Islam in the twelfth century. This flag was used from 1958 to 1962 by the provisional government of the Algerian Republic during Algeria's war for independence. It was officially adopted when Algeria became an independent country on July 3, 1962.**

# Geography

Algeria covers an area of 919,595 square miles (2,381,740 square kilometers). The country is located in northwest Africa, in an area known as the Maghrib. Algeria is bordered to the north by the Mediterranean Sea, to the east by Tunisia and Libya, to the south by Niger and Mali, and to the west by Morocco, Mauritania and a small piece of Western Sahara. About 80 percent of Algeria is made up of the vast Sahara Desert.

The majority of Algeria's population lives in the north of the country, along the Mediterranean coast, in inland valleys, and on plateaus. The Saharan Atlas Mountains extend between northeastern Algeria and the Sahara Desert region. The Tell Atlas Mountains run east to west across northern Algeria. The Sahara Desert lies to the south of the country. Algeria's coastline, which is rocky and dotted with bays and inlets, is 620 miles (998 kilometers) long. Three of Algeria's largest cities — Algiers, Annaba, and Oran — are located along the Mediterranean coast and serve as the country's major ports.

*Below:* **The beautiful Aurès Mountains are located in northeastern Algeria. They are home to northern Algeria's highest peak, Mount Chélia, which is 7,638 feet (2,328 m) high. The Aurès Mountains are part of the Saharan Atlas Mountains.**

*Left:* **The Algerian Sahara consists of miles of sand dunes.**

## The Tell and the High Plateau

The Tell is the northernmost region of Algeria. It is home to most of Algeria's population and most of the country's agricultural land. The Tell includes hills, plains, valleys, basins, and the Tell Atlas Mountains. Located south of these mountains is a region known as the High Plateau. The High Plateau is a semiarid, featureless plain that is covered in some places by a coarse type of grass known as esparto grass. Esparto grass is used to make paper, ropes, and baskets.

The Chelif River is the country's longest and most important river. The Chelif River runs a course of 450 miles (725 km), beginning in the Saharan Atlas Mountains, flowing north across the High Plateau and the Tell Atlas Mountains, and finally draining into the Mediterranean Sea.

## The Sahara

The Sahara, the world's largest desert, lies south of the High Plateau. The Algerian Sahara is divided into two regions: the Great Western Erg and the Great Eastern Erg. The Great Eastern Erg consists of large areas of sand dunes, which can be up to 15 feet (5 meters) high. The Great Eastern Erg is home to sand dunes and the Ahaggar Mountains, which contain Algeria's highest peak, Mount Tahat, at 9,573 feet (3,003 m).

### ERGS

Ergs, or sand seas, are vast areas of sand in a desert. Ergs consists of shifting sand dunes, or large sheets of sand. The Great Western Erg and the Great Eastern Erg are difficult to cross because they are made of loose, shifting sand.

# Climate

The climate in Algeria ranges from a mild, Mediterranean climate in the northern coastal parts of the country to a scorching desert climate in the south. The Tell region experiences warm, dry summers, with temperatures averaging between 70° Fahrenheit (21° Celsius) and 75° F (24° C). Winters are mild, with average temperatures between 50° F (10° C) and 54° F (12° C), but are humid and rainy. Precipitation is highest along the Mediterranean coast and decreases southward.

The High Plateau, in the Tell region, experiences more extreme temperature variations. Temperatures can soar to 100° F (38° C) in the summer and can drop to near freezing in winter. The High Plateau is also subject to a seasonal hot, sandy wind called a sirocco. This choking wind blows from the Sahara Desert in the summer, sometimes reaching as far north as the Tell. When this happens, it makes life unpleasant for people in the Tell. Sometimes, the sirocco blows with gale force.

The Sahara Desert has a typical desert climate. Daytime temperatures are often higher than those of the High Plateau, with rapidly falling temperatures at sunset. Precipitation is irregular, and some parts of the Sahara Desert have not recorded rainfall in many years.

## THE TUAREGS

The Tuaregs, also called "the Blue Men" because of their indigo-colored head covers, are a nomadic Berber people who live in the Algerian Sahara Desert and other parts of North Africa. They are known for their ability to withstand the scorching desert heat.
*(A Closer Look, page 72)*

*Left:* **Coastal areas in Algeria have a warm Mediterranean climate, which supports the cultivation of crops.**

*Left:* **The scimitar oryx is a type of antelope that lives in Africa. It has a pale coat and long, slender horns. The animal became extinct in Algeria in 1996.**

## Plants and Animals

Only about 2 percent of Algeria is occupied by forests. Algeria's forests are found in the country's mountain regions. These forests contain pine, cedar, oak, and juniper trees. The Tell used to be covered with woodland, but the vegetation in the region today consists mostly of shrubs, such as laurel, rosemary, and gorse. These shrubs are found on the lower slopes of mountains. The High Plateau supports hardier plants, such as brushwood and esparto grass, that grow in scattered clumps. In the Sahara Desert, only desert grass and drought-resistant plants, such as acacia, tamarisk, and jujube trees, can be found. These stunted and often spiny trees need very little water to survive.

Because of Algeria's sparse vegetation, the country supports a limited variety of animal life. Algeria's northern mountain regions are home to wild boars and Barbary apes. The Algerian Sahara Desert sustains hyenas, jackals, vultures, gazelles, snakes, and lizards. Two of Algeria's indigenous animals, the scimitar oryx and dama gazelle, became extinct in Algeria in 1996. Algeria also has about four hundred species of birds. The Algerian nuthatch, discovered in 1975, however, is the only bird species found only in Algeria, and it is endangered. Migratory birds, including flamingos, pass through Algeria each year.

# History

Human beings are believed to have inhabited Northern Africa more than 200,000 years ago. At Tassili n'Ajjer in Algeria, prehistoric cave paintings that date from between 6000 B.C. and A.D. 1 depict the daily lives of the region's early inhabitants. Over time, the various inhabitants of the region collectively became known as Berbers. The Berbers developed a distinct culture and language that survives today. They are regarded as the first Algerians.

## Under Carthage and Rome

In 800 B.C., the Phoenicians, a seagoing people from the area that is present-day Lebanon, established a colony at Carthage, which is in the area that is now Tunisia. The Phoenicians established settlements along the North African coast. Many of Algeria's coastal cities and towns began as Carthaginian trading outposts. The Carthaginians traded with the Berbers, but periodic Berber revolts and the three wars — known as the Punic Wars — fought with Rome in the second and third centuries B.C. weakened Carthaginian power. In 146 B.C., Carthage fell to the Romans, and the Berber kingdoms began to flourish. By A.D. 24, however, the Romans controlled almost all Berber territory.

**TASSILI N'AJJER**

The site of prehistoric rock paintings, Tassili n'Ajjer not only has cultural significance but is also important geologically.
(*A Closer Look, page 70*)

*Left*: **An Algerian man looks at a prehistoric cave painting at Tassili n'Ajjer that depicts a rhinoceros. Some cave paintings show a variety of animals that used to live in Algeria, including elephants and buffalo.**

*Above:* **Ancient Roman ruins still stand at Timgad. Today, they attract tourists and archaeologists.**

The region flourished under Roman rule. The Romans built impressive cities, including Djémila and Timgad. These cities were a major source of grain and olive oil for the entire Roman Empire. Towns dependent on agriculture prospered. The Berbers, however, were driven into what is now the Algerian interior when their land was confiscated by the Romans for crop cultivation. The Berbers constantly opposed the Romans, forcing the Romans to construct a line of forts in the hinterland as a defense against Berber attacks.

## The Vandals

The Vandals, a Christian Germanic people, ruled the region that is present-day northern Tunisia and northeastern Algeria from A.D. 429 to A.D. 534. In A.D. 439, they captured Carthage from the Romans and established their own government in the region. Vandal rule ended when they were defeated by the Byzantines, and Rome regained control of the region.

**CITY OF CONSTANTINE**

Fortified by nature, the city of Constantine has been ruled by people from various lands. Constantine has an intriguing history and is still a thriving city today.

(*A Closer Look, page 50*)

*Left:* **This woodcut illustrates the European attack on Algiers led by Charles V in 1541.**

## The Islamic Conquest

The Arabs brought Islam into North Africa in A.D. 642, when Arab armies reached the Maghrib. The Berbers began converting to Islam, but many Christians and Jews living in the region resisted Islam. By A.D. 711, all of North Africa had came under Arab Muslim rule.

In the late fifteenth century, Algeria's Ottoman rulers, who were known as deys, began to hire privateers to raid European ships in the Mediterranean. Privateers were independent ship captains who raided ships and shared the spoils with the deys. Many European states paid a fee, known as a tribute, to Algeria to guarantee safe passage for their ships. Nonetheless, privateers were the main source of income for the deys, and the city of Algiers became the privateers' principal stronghold.

Europe and the United States resented the North African privateers. In 1815, Algeria engaged in a naval war with the United States, Spain, Russia, and other European countries. Algeria suffered a defeat in 1816 after a fleet, made up of British and Dutch ships, bombarded Algiers for nine hours. This attack forced the deys to sign a treaty that ended privateering as well as the practice of taking Christians as slaves.

### RED BEARD

Khayr Ad-Din (c. 1483–1546), known to the Europeans as Barbarossa or "Red Beard," and his brother Aruj were notorious Muslim privateers. Red Beard captured Algiers in 1529, and the city became the center for piracy along the Mediterranean coast. Red Beard was also an Ottoman admiral. Algeria and Tunisia became part of the Ottoman Empire because of his military leadership and skills. Algeria was part of the Ottoman Empire until 1830.

# French Algeria and the Struggle for Independence

In 1830, France invaded and captured Algiers. By 1834, Algeria had become a French colony. Thousand of Europeans — mainly Spanish, French, and Italians — settled in Algeria. The French *colons* (KO-lens), or colonists, confiscated farmland from the locals and seized religious buildings. The locals became increasingly unhappy with the French, and in 1871, they led an uprising against them, which the French suppressed. Algerians were also saddled with heavier taxes and granted fewer privileges than the European colonists. A reformist movement began in 1892 to protest against these French policies. By the 1940s, Algerians had formed several political organizations but faced strong opposition from the European colonists.

After World War II, a group of nine Algerian leaders formed a political party called the Front de Libération Nationale (FLN). On November 1, 1954, the FLN launched a guerilla war, later called the Algerian War of Independence, against the colonists and the French army. France also experienced increasing international pressure to grant Algeria its independence. In 1959, the French president, Charles de Gaulle, declared that Algerians had the right to determine their own future. This angered the colonists and led to an unsuccessful rebellion against de Gaulle. In May 1961, de Gaulle completed independence negotiations with the FLN. Algeria was declared an independent country on July 3, 1962.

**THE BATTLE OF ALGIERS**

Released in the mid 1960s, *The Battle of Algiers* is a movie depicting how a group of Algerians fought for independence from the French. Based on true events, the film won a number of international awards. *(A Closer Look, page 44)*

*Left:* **A confrontation between French security forces and Muslim demonstrators led to the deaths of at least sixty people during a 1960 revolt in Algiers.**

# Independent Algeria

Ahmed Ben Bella (1918– ) was Algeria's first prime minister and first elected president. Under his leadership, Algeria adopted a socialist economy. In 1965, Ben Bella was overthrown in a coup d'etat by Houari Boumedienne (1927–1978), who took over as the country's president. Boumedienne focused on the country's economic problems, resulting in Algeria's rapid industrialization. Boumedienne died in 1978 and was replaced by Chadli Bendjedid, a colonel and former guerilla officer.

In the 1980s, Algeria faced an economic crisis when oil prices fell. The country's leaders introduced a new constitution that did away with socialism and legalized political parties. Frustrated Algerians rallied around the Front Islamique du Salut (FIS), a political party that wanted to rule Algeria by strict Islamic law. In 1991, the FIS stunned the world by winning the nationwide elections. Soon after the FIS victory, the Algerian army declared the elections void and seized control of the country.

# Civil War and Civil Unrest

The FIS and its allies responded by launching a violent rebellion against the Algerian army. From 1992 to 1998, nearly 100,000 Algerians — most of whom were civilians — were killed either by Islamic fighters or by Algerian security forces. In 1999, Abdelaziz Bouteflika was elected president and promised to restore national harmony, but incidents of violence and terrorism continued.

*Left:* **The bodies of victims of a terrorist attack lie in coffins ready to be buried. The attack took place in a small town near Algiers in 2001. It was carried out by a militant Islamic group.**

## Abd al Qadir (1808–1883)

Abd al Qadir led the opposition against the French occupation of Algeria in the 1830s. Algerians regard him as a hero of Algerian independence for his efforts in resisting the French. Al Qadir died in Damascus, Syria, in 1883. In 1966, the government transferred his remains from Syria to Algeria for a ceremonial burial. A mosque in the province of Constantine bears his name and is a national shrine.

Djamila Bouhired

## Djamila Bouhired (1935– )

Djamila Bouhired joined Algeria's underground independence movement, as a part of which she became involved in guerilla activities in Algiers. In 1957, she was captured by the French, tortured, and condemned to death. Her execution was postponed, and she was jailed instead. In 1962, she was released from prison when Algeria won its independence. Some Algerians regard her as a freedom fighter and a national heroine.

## Ahmed Ben Bella (1918– )

Ahmed Ben Bella was a major figure in the Algerian War of Independence. As one of the leaders of the FLN, Ben Bella helped to organize the rebellion against French colonial rule, acquire arms, and gather international support for its cause. In 1963, Ben Bella was elected Algeria's first president. Ben Bella was popular with Algerians, but his increasing abuse of power finally led to his downfall, and he was ousted from office and arrested. In 1980, Ben Bella was freed. He returned to Algeria in 1990, after spending ten years in exile.

Ahmed Ben Bella

## Houari Boumedienne (1927–1978)

Houari Boumedienne was the minister of defense during the presidency of Ahmed Ben Bella. He became Algeria's second president in 1965 after ousting Ben Bella but initially received little public support. During his presidency, he resolved internal divisions within his regime, resulting in a single-party government that was dominated by the FLN. Boumedienne focused on the country's economic growth and is credited with modernizing Algeria.

Houari Boumedienne

# Government and the Economy

Algeria is a republic. The president of the country is elected by popular vote to serve a five-year term and can run for reelection only once. The president appoints the prime minister and the cabinet, controls the country's armed forces, and has the power to dissolve the country's parliament. In 1999, Abdelaziz Bouteflika became Algeria's president, after winning over 70 percent of the vote. The six candidates who ran against him dropped out of the elections because they claimed that the electoral process was fraudulent. Bouteflika was relected to a second term in 2004.

Algeria's parliament consists of the 389-seat National People's Assembly, whose members are elected by popular vote to serve five-year terms, and the 144-seat Council of Nations. The president appoints one-third of the members of the Council of Nations and the remaining members are elected by regional councils to serve six-year terms. Algeria has fourteen political parties. The FIS, however, has been outlawed since 1992.

## FRONT DE LIBÉRATION NATIONALE (FLN)

The FLN played a main role in Algeria's stuggle for independence against the French. For more than thirty years, the FLN was the only political party in the country's government.
*(A Closer Look, page 56)*

*Left:* Abdelaziz Bouteflika waves to a crowd of supporters during the 1999 election in which he won Algeria's presidency. In April 2004, Bouteflika was relected to a second five-year term.

## Legal System

Algeria's legal system combines Islamic religious law, socialist principles, and French secular law. The Supreme Court, located in Algiers, is the highest court in the land, with judges appointed by the executive branch.

Algeria has a special legal body, called the Constitutional Council, that has the task of ensuring that all acts of parliament, treaties, and regulations are consistent with Algeria's constitution. The Constitutional Council also reports the results of legislative and presidential elections.

## Regional Government

Algeria is divided into 48 *wilayat* (wee-LIE-yat), or provinces. Each wilaya is governed by a provincial assembly consisting of thirty elected deputies and headed by a *wali* (WAH-lee), or governor. The president appoints walis who serve as the main links between the people living in the provinces and the government located in Algiers. The provincial governments are in charge of distributing the services provided by the national government, creating new government companies, and regulating agriculture, educational institutions, small and medium enterprises, road transportation, and tourism.

**ALGERIA'S CONSTITUTION**

Algeria has had two separate constitutions since its independence. The first one, which lasted for only two years, was drawn up in 1963 and established Algeria as a socialist republic. Between 1965 and 1976, Algeria did not have a constitution. In November 1976, a new constitution was drawn up and accepted by a referendum. This consitution has been revised three times — in 1988, 1989, and 1996.

# The Economy

The government-controlled oil and gas industries are the most important sectors of the Algerian economy. Every year, Algeria exports billions of dollars of oil and gas to the United States, Italy, Spain, and France. The earnings from oil and gas sales account for over 60 percent of the Algerian government's annual national budget and 30 percent of the country's annual gross domestic product (GDP). Algeria's reliance on oil and gas sales leaves it at the mercy of changes in global oil and gas prices. When these prices fall, the Algerian economy suffers.

The agricultural sector accounts for about 8 percent of Algeria's GDP and employs 25 percent of the country's population. The country's agricultural products include wheat, barley, oats, grapes, olives, and citrus fruit. Algeria is not self-sufficient and has to import some of its food.

Algeria's economy is moving toward becoming a market-driven economy with an increasing number of privately owned businesses. The Algerian government has tried to encourage foreign investment in industries other than oil and gas in an effort to develop new industries and to diversify the Algerian economy. Their efforts, however, have met with little success because war and violence have discouraged many foreign companies from investing in Algeria.

**THE ENGINE OF ALGERIA'S ECONOMY**

**The economy of Algeria is heavily dependent on the country's oil and gas industries.**
*(A Closer Look, page 52)*

*Left:* **Markets in Algeria sell the country's fresh produce, from fruits and vegetables to meat.**

As a result, Algeria suffers from severe economic problems. Nearly a quarter of Algerians live below the poverty line, and unemployment stands at over 30 percent. The Algerians most affected by poverty and unemployment are the rural population. In 2003, the World Bank approved a loan of U.S. $95 million to the Algerian government to help raise the living standards of Algeria's rural population and to help generate employment opportunities for them.

*Left:* **Algeria has thirteen ports. The ports at Algiers (*top*), Annaba, and Oran are the country's three largest.**

## Transportation

Algeria's road system consists of 64,640 miles (104,000 km) of paved and unpaved roads. The road network is more developed in the densely populated northern coastal regions. Three major east–west highways run from Algeria to Tunisia and Morocco. The Trans-Saharan Road, also known as the "Road of African Unity," runs from Algeria's Mediterranean coast across the Sahara Desert to Algeria's southern borders with Niger and Mali.

Algeria has over 54 airports. The country's national airline, Air Algérie, provides both international and domestic flights. International airports can be found in the Algerian cities of Algiers, Annaba, Constantine, Oran, Tlemcen, and Ghardaïa.

# People and Lifestyle

Algeria has a population of almost 32 million people, most of whom are Berbers and Arabs. The Berbers are the country's original inhabitants, and many Berbers still maintain their ethnic identity, language, and cultural traditions. Over the centuries, the other cultures that invaded and colonized Algeria, such as the Romans, Arabs and the French, intermarried with the Berbers. As a result, almost every Algerian today has some Berber heritage. The vast majority of Algerians, however, consider themselves Arabs.

Although Algeria's birth rate has declined in recent years, the country still has a comparatively youthful population. About 33 percent of Algerians are under the age of fifteen, as opposed to about 20 percent in both France and the United States. The country's population growth rate is about 1.7 percent. Algeria's population is expected to exceed 40 million by 2025.

**THE BERBERS FIGHT BACK**

Berbers were one of the first peoples who lived in North Africa. Over time, the Berbers have fought to retain their identity, culture and language.
*(A Closer Look, page 46)*

*Below:* About 4 percent of Algeria's population is over 65 years old. The life expectancy of male Algerians is about 69 years, while the life expectancy of female Algerians is 72 years.

*Left:* Laundry is hung out to dry in the narrow backlanes of shantytowns in Algeria. These run-down homes house the rural poor who come to cities in search of work and a better life.

## Urbanization

About half of Algeria's population today lives in urban areas. Every year, migrants move from rural areas — where jobs and opportunities are scarce — to the major cities, most of which lie along the Mediterranean coast in the north. Migration to the cities has led to numerous problems, such as overcrowding, urban unemployment, and a decrease in agricultural output. Algeria has had a severe urban housing shortage since the 1970s. In the 1980s, Algeria's government tried to slow urban migration with programs aimed at improving the quality of rural life, but unrest in the rural areas still drives people to move to the cities. It is estimated that Algeria's urban population will increase. Algeria's capital city, Algiers, is the country's largest urban area, with a population of about 1.8 million people.

## Algerian Homes

Housing in Algeria is varied. Wealthy urban Algerians live in private houses or modern apartment buildings. Many poor Algerians live in the shantytowns of the country's cities. In the rural areas, the most common dwelling is the *gourbi* (GUR-bee), a hut made of mud and branches. More elaborate gourbi have walls made of stone or clay and a flat tiled or tin roof.

# Family Life

Traditional Algerian society is based on the extended family, which includes grandparents, their married sons and families, unmarried sons and daughters, and other relatives, often living close to one another or in the same house. The family lives under the authority of the oldest male, who makes all the major decisions. The traditional family structure in Algeria is changing as the country becomes more urbanized. Although family ties remain strong, the tradition of male elders' authority has weakened, because more Algerians are living in separate nuclear family units. One reason for this change is that the housing in urban areas is more suited to smaller families rather than large, extended families. Well-educated Algerians also prefer to live independently from their parents and have fewer children.

In many parts of rural Algeria, especially among the Berbers, the extended family remains the most important social unit. Women in traditional Algerian society live under male authority and do not work outside the home. Their main responsibilities are tending to the household and taking care of the children.

*Below:* **This public housing complex is home to many small Algerian families. Most of the housing in Algeria is occupied, and the country faces a housing shortage.**

*Left:* **Algerian women and children in the city of Bab el-Oued.**

# Women and Marriage

In Algerian society, marriage is based on Islamic law. Many Algerian women have arranged marriages. Traditionally, the bride's family negotiates an agreement with the groom's family to determine the terms of the marriage and the conditions under which the marriage may be terminated. The wedding celebrations may last several days. Once the couple is married, the woman leaves her family and moves to her husband's home.

The average marrying ages for men and women in Algeria have increased. Young Algerian men find it harder to settle down because of the housing shortage in many Algerian cities and the country's high unemployment rate. The financial difficulty faced by many young Algerian men is one factor that has contributed to a rise in the number of single Algerian women. In 2002, about 51 percent of Algerian women were unmarried.

Algerian women are also having fewer children. In the 1970s, an Algerian woman gave birth to an average of seven or eight children. Today, the number has declined sharply to two or three children per woman. A woman's status in her husband's household increases if she bears a son. As a result, Algerian women tend to favor sons over daughters.

**THE STATUS AND RIGHTS OF WOMEN**

In Algerian society, women are subjected to the laws laid down by the Family Code, which regards all women as minors.
*(A Closer Look, page 68)*

# Education

Only 70 percent of Algerians over the age of fifteen can read and write. The literacy rate is higher among men than women, which is a reflection of the traditional role that women are expected to play in Algerian society.

Under French colonial rule, French was the language of instruction in Algerian schools. Before 1949, separate schools existed for French and Algerian children, but many Algerian children did not attend school at all. After independence, the Algerian government launched an intensive program to improve the country's education system to suit the needs of the country and to promote Arab culture. Arabic replaced French as the language of instruction.

Nine years of primary and middle school education are compulsory for all Algerian children, and education is free. Students move on to the secondary, or high school, level, where they can choose to pursue either general, specialized, or vocational training. Students must pass the Baccalauréate examination in order to graduate from secondary school. They may then enroll in a university, technical institute, or vocational training center.

In 1996, Algeria had about 350,000 students enrolled in the country's universities, technical institutes, specialized institutes, and teacher training institutes. In 1999, about 423,000 students were enrolled in the country's universities.

*Left:* Algerian children begin attending primary school at six years old. They are taught in Arabic. They learn French as a second language later. Children in Algerian public schools must also study Islam. In 1962, the country's literacy rate was less than 10 percent. Today, it has increased to 70 percent.

Algeria has ten universities, but the most prominent are the University of Oran, the University of Science and Technology at Oran, the University of Constantine, and the University of Algiers. Some young Algerians pursue higher education in Europe, Canada, or the United States. In 1989, adult education became possible at ten regional institutes in the country. This allows working Algerians to resume their studies or pursue higher degrees.

## Education for Women

The educational opportunites for Algerian girls have steadily improved since the country's independence in 1962. Women account for about 40 percent of the student population from primary to college levels. In urban areas, such as Algiers, girls and boys receive virtually the same level of education. In rural areas, however, girls are less likely to attend school for the same number of years as boys.

Many Algerian women attend universities, but only about 7 percent of Algeria's workforce are women. Those that pursue professional careers usually work as teachers, doctors, and nurses.

*Above:* **Before independence, Algeria's schools were staffed by teachers from France. Today, most of Algeria's 340,000 teachers are Algerians, but their numbers remain insufficient. In 2002, the Algerian government raised the salary for teachers as part of efforts to improve the country's education system.**

## Islam

The Arabs brought Islam to the region in the seventh and eighth centuries. By the tenth century, most of North Africa was Muslim. Today, Muslims make up over 99 percent of Algeria's population, and Islam is Algeria's official religion. Islam has two branches: Sunni and Shi'ite. Algerians are Sunni Muslims.

Mosques, which are Islamic houses of worship, are found throughout Algeria. Muslims answer the call to prayer from a religious official called a muezzin five times a day. On Friday, the Islamic holy day, Muslims assemble in mosques to pray. Some Algerian Muslims, especially urban dwellers and the younger generations, practice a liberal version of Islam.

After Algeria's independence, the Algerian government used Islam to unite the country. They made Islam the state religion and partially based Algerian law on Islamic law. The government built mosques, funded religious institutes, and appointed religious leaders. Some conservative Islamic groups want Islam to play a larger role in Algerian government and society. They oppose what they believe are Western practices in Algerian society. The tension between this group and those who are more liberal in their interpretation of Islam has been the cause of civil unrest and terrorist violence in Algeria today.

*Top:* **Muslims pray five times a day. During their prayers, Muslims kneel in the direction of Mecca, a city in Saudi Arabia.**

**THE FIVE PILLARS OF ISLAM**

**Devout Muslims are expected to observe five guidelines, known as the Five Pillars of Islam. Muslims must profess faith in their God, Allah, and in the prophet Muhammad, pray five times a day, give alms to the poor, and fast during the holy month of Ramadan. Finally, Muslims must go on a pilgrimage to the holy city of Mecca, in Saudi Arabia. Muslims are also prohibited from eating pork or drinking alcohol.**

# Jews and Christians

Less than one percent of Algeria's population are Jews or Christians. For several centuries, Algeria was home to a fairly large Jewish community. When Algeria achieved independence in 1962, most of the 140,000 Algerian Jews left the country because they felt discriminated against by the Algerian government. Today, it is believed that fewer than one hundred Jews live in Algeria.

Algeria's Christian community is predominantly made up of 25,000 Roman Catholics and a small number of Protestants. Christianity was brought to the region by the Romans but gradually waned in influence after the Arab invasion. It was reintroduced during French colonial rule. After the country's independence, many Christians left Algeria because of civil unrest. Those who remained in Algeria live in the larger cities of Algiers, Constantine, and Oran.

Algerian law limits the extent non-Muslim faiths can be practiced but allows Christian religious services to be conducted. Many Christians conduct their religious services either in small churches or at home.

**THE JEWS OF ALGERIA**

When Algeria was a French colony, Jews in the country numbered well over one hundred thousand. Today, there are fewer than one hundred of them left in the country.
(*A Closer Look, page 58*)

**SAINT AUGUSTINE OF HIPPO**

A well-known saint of the Roman Catholic Church, Saint Augustine wrote many works that have been used as the foundation for modern Christian thought.
(*A Closer Look, page 66*)

*Left:* **The cathedral of Notre Dame d'Afrique is located in Algiers.**

# Language and Literature

## Official and Native Languages

When Algeria became independent, the government was eager to break away from French influence. The country's new constitution made Arabic the official language of Algeria. The Arabization Law dictated that Arabic must be used for all official business dealings with the government. The law also required that the official language be used in all television and radio broadcasts and that all foreign language films must be dubbed or subtitled in Arabic. Prescriptions for medicine and labels on communication equipment must also carry translations in Arabic.

In addition to Arabic, Algeria recognizes two other languages: French and Tamazight, the main language of the Berbers. In 1991, about 83 percent of the total population spoke Arabic. In 1993, about 20 percent of the country's population was literate in French, although a larger percentage was able only to speak the language. About 14 percent of all Algerians speak Tamazight or one of its dialects.

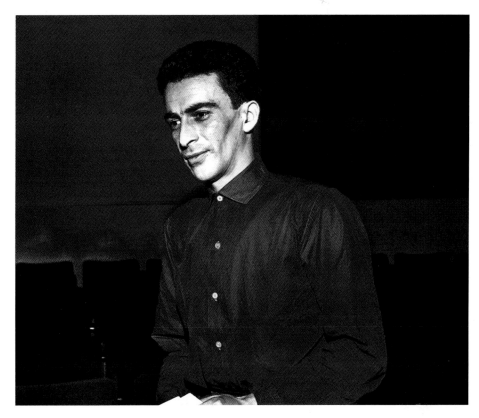

*Left:* A well-respected literary personality, Kateb Yacine was an author, a playwright, and a poet. Growing up during Algeria's colonial period, he was educated in French. Some of Yacine's literary works were written in French. His plays, however, were written in Arabic. Yacine's first novel, *Nedjma* (1956), is a classic that has influenced the growth of French-language North African literature.

## Algerian Literature

The Berber language has the longest history of any language in Algeria because its original speakers, the Berbers, were the first inhabitants of the country. Colonization brought the Arabic and French languages to the country. As a result, Algerian literature includes works written in Arabic, French, and Berber.

In the beginning, stories were passed down through an oral tradition and in poetry. The French colonizers introduced the novel to Algerian literature. The various themes covered in novels by Algerian writers include the country's struggle to break away from colonial rule, Algeria's fight for independence, and Islam in Algerian society. Authors such as Mouloud Feraoun (1913–1962) wrote about the cultural heritage of the Berbers.

Some well-known Algerian literary figures include Mouloud Mammeri (1917–1989), Mohammed Dib (1920–2003), Jean Sénac (1926–1973), Kateb Yacine (1929–1989), Rachid Mimouni (1945–1995), and Rachid Boujedra (1941– ).

Albert Camus (1913–1960) and Assia Djebar (1936– ) are Algerian writers who have won international awards for their contributions to world literature.

### FEMINIST ASSIA DJEBAR

Assia Djebar is a well-known and talented Algerian playwright, novelist, poet, and filmmaker. Most of her works deal with women and their plight.

*(A Closer Look, page 54)*

### ALBERT CAMUS

A Nobel laureate, Albert Camus was a novelist and playwright who used his own experiences in Algeria as a backdrop for his works.

*(A Closer Look, page 48)*

*Opposite:* Arabic is Algeria's official language, but many Algerians were educated in French. Street signs in the country are written in both Arabic and French.

# Arts

## Music

Algerian music has roots in the musical traditions of a number of cultures. One such tradition is Andalusian classical music, which comes from the courts of Moorish Spain. It was introduced into Algeria by the Spanish Moors, Arabs, and Jews who were expelled from Spain. Algiers, Constantine and Tlemcen were the cities where Andalusian music was most influential. In Algiers and Tlemcen, this style had strong Arab influences.

The music of the Berber desert nomads, who sing of love, heroes and their courageous deeds, and sadness, reflects the barren nature of their surroundings. Normally, the songs use only a single drum and vocals. The music of some of the Berber and Arab nomadic groups is characterized by high-pitched singing of female vocalists accompanied by the clapping of hands. Another form of traditional desert music is created using various wind instruments and has a haunting sound.

*Below:* **A Berber villager from the town of Tindouf plays a traditional stringed instrument. To ensure the growth and continuity of traditional folklore, music, and dance, Algeria's National Institute of Music conducts programs that teach these art forms to future generations.**

The Berbers have a tradition of folk music that is sung in their own language. Berber folk music gained popularity outside Algeria through the works of musicians such as Lounés Matoub (1956–1998) and Idir (1955– ). Both of these musicians have used their music to protest against Arabization by the Algerian government and to promote Berber culture and its way of life.

The style of Arab folk music that began in the city of Algiers is known as *chaabi* (CHA-bee). Today, chaabi has become a form of urban popular music. Many chaabi songs have traditional themes of love and duty. Chaabi lyrics also speak of changes in society and in the country. Some chaabi musicians sing about varied subjects, such as migration and the current conflicts facing Algeria. One of the most well-known chaabi musicians was El Hajj Muhammad El Anka (d. 1978).

*Rai* (RYE) is another form of music that has its origins in Algeria. Rai music has a strong, danceable rhythm and evolved from the traditional practice of singing poetry. *Wahrani* (wah-RAN-i) is a style of rai music that blends the sounds of the accordion with instruments from the percussion, string, and flute families.

*Above:* **Berber musician Lounés Matoub used music to express his discontent with the Algerian government's attempts to suppress the Berber culture. In 1976, he cofounded the Algerian Human Rights League. In 1978, he migrated to France but continued his protest through music. In 1998, Matoub returned to Algeria for a visit and was killed in an ambush.**

### RAI MUSIC

**Rai has its roots in traditional folk music. Over time, rai music has evolved. Today, rai music combines musical traditions and highlights bold and often controversial lyrics.**
*(A Closer Look, page 64)*

## Architectural Heritage

Algeria boasts a rich architectual heritage because of the various cultures that have controlled the country. The country's architectural legacy includes Turkish palaces, Roman ruins, and Arab mosques. Many great buildings can be found within the capital city of Algiers. French cathedrals stand next to Turkish palaces and houses. An area known as the Kasbah was declared a World Heritage site by the United Nations Educational, Scientific, and Cultural Organization (UNESCO). The Kasbah has narrow, zigzagging streets lined by traditional houses.

The Romans built a number of cities in the country during their rule. The well-preserved ruins of these cities still exist today, giving Algeria the greatest ruins in North Africa. Roman ruins are found in the cities of Djémila, Timgad, and Tipasa. In 2001, Algeria received a grant from the U.S. Ambassadors' Fund for Cultural Preservation to preserve Roman mosaics at Cherchell, a town west of Algiers.

The oasis town of El Oued has been called the "Town of a Thousand Domes" because of the domed roofs of its clay houses. Roman and Moorish influences can be seen in the city's mosques.

**THE LEGACY OF ROME**

The Romans dominated North Africa for more than five centuries. Certain towns in Algeria were centers of Roman activity. To this day, some of these towns still hold the remains of this once powerful empire.
*(A Closer Look, page 62)*

**THE KASBAH OF ALGIERS**

Located in the city of Algiers, the Kasbah was declared a UNESCO World Heritage site in 1992. Today, the section is undergoing restoration.
*(A Closer Look, page 60)*

# Handicrafts

Algeria has a flourishing handicrafts industry. In an effort to preserve and promote traditional methods of craft making, the government constructed handicraft centers. Local artisans can make carpets, jewelry, pottery, embroidered pieces, and brass metalwork at these centers.

Algerian carpets are woven using traditional methods. One of Algeria's centers for carpet making is the town of Ghardaïa. Algerian rugs are brightly colored and come in a variety of sizes. They are used as prayer mats, saddle rugs, bath mats, and foot rugs. The carpets made in rural areas have deeper and bolder colors and are usually used as blankets on cold nights.

Algeria has a rich tradition in jewelry making that has been influenced by both the Berbers and the Arabs. Using the traditional techniques of the Ottoman Turks, exquisite items are created from sheets of copper. Algerian copperwork artisans are found in the cities of Algiers, Ghardaïa, Tlemcen, Tindouf, and Constantine.

*Opposite:* **The Arch of Trajan is one of the Roman ruins in the ancient city of Timgad. Excavations at the site began in 1881. The remains at the site are among the largest ruins that are still in good condition. The city is sometimes known as the "Pompeii of North Africa."**

*Left:* **Algerian carpets are made using sheep's wool, goats' hair, and even camels' hair. The patterns on the carpets vary from one region to another. One popular pattern is a broad cross against a background of subtle colors. One of Algeria's renowned writers, Mohammed Dib, once worked in the carpet industry in Tlemcen.**

33

# Leisure and Festivals

## How Algerians Relax

In Algerian society, traditional values based on Islam are strong. Family is important, and men play a leading role in all major decisions. Women tend to stay in the background. As a result, the women's social lives are centered around the home, and their interaction is limited to other female members of the family.

Algerian men often go to cafés to meet with their friends for a game of chess, checkers, or dominoes. Some men enjoy visiting the public baths, which are known as *hammams*. The public bath was a common social area for the Romans and the Turks, and hammams played an important role in Roman and Turkish society. Today, Algerian men still visit hammams to relax in steam baths or pools and to catch up with their friends.

*Below:* **Many Algerians live according to the Islamic teachings that forbid women from socializing outside of their familes and in public. In the cities, it is not unusual to find groups of men at a café playing board games, enjoying a hot drink together, and chatting with no women around.**

Left: Algerian children
are brought up by
all members of the
family. The country's
strong oral tradition
has been kept alive
by women who pass
down stories about
important social and
historical events, such
as marriages, births,
and even droughts.

Algeria's coastline is the home to beach resorts, especially near the cities of Algiers, Annaba, and Oran. During the summer, especially in the month of August, Algerian families vacation at resorts where they can sail, water ski, or swim.

## Relaxing in the Desert

Algerians living in the desert relax in a different manner. Horse and camel racing are popular pastimes. In one variation of Algerian racing sports, horseback riders are required to aim at and shoot a target while riding their horses at top speed. The horses then have to be brought to a full stop.

Camel dancing is a recreational sport performed at certain festivals. Riders show off their skills by moving their camels in time with the beat of traditional music. In certain parts of the Sahara Desert, desert dwellers enjoy skiing on the sand.

## CHILDREN AT PLAY

One popular Algerian children's game uses a snake-like shape that is drawn on the street or sidewalk and divided into twenty numbered boxes. Five of the boxes are marked as "jails." The game can be played in teams or individually. In each turn, a player throws one bottle cap into a box, starting with the box with the lowest number. In the next turn, a bottle cap is thrown into the next highest numbered box. The object of the game is to be the first to reach the twentieth box. Other players, however, may try to stop that from happening by knocking away their opponent's bottle caps, making the thrower start from the first box again. In the event that a bottle cap lands on a box marked "jail," a thrower will also have to start again from box one.

# Soccer

Soccer ranks first among all the sports enjoyed by Algerians. In the international arena, the national team has earned a strong reputation. Since 1970, it has participated in nine successive World Cup competitions, qualifying for the tournament in 1982 and 1986. The Algerian team, however, failed to get past the first round. The team is currently forty-third in world rankings.

Algeria has an even stronger standing in soccer among the African nations. In the 1990 African Nations Cup, the country beat Nigeria to take home the trophy. In the 2004 championships, Algeria surprised fans by scoring against Egypt, a four-time winner of the African Nations Cup. The Algerian team made it to the quarter-finals but failed to win their match with Morocco.

One of the most renowned Algerian personalities in soccer is Zinedine Zidane. Of Berber descent, Zidane was born in Marseilles and began his career by playing in French clubs and leagues. He played on the team that helped France win the World Cup in 1998. Currently, Zidane is a midfielder for Spain's Real Madrid team. In 2003, Zidane was voted Player of the Year by the Fédération Internationale de Football Association (FIFA) for the third time. He previously received this honor in 1998 and 2000.

*Below:* In Algeria, soccer is so popular that children begin playing the sport at an early age. A favorite spectator sport among Algerians, matches involving the national team usually have many fans with drums and trumpets in the stands.

*Left:* Athlete Hassiba Boulmerka (1968– ) has achieved a number of victories for Algeria. In 1991, she became the first African woman to win a gold medal at the World Athletics Championships. In 1992, she was the first Algerian to win a gold medal at the Olympics held in Barcelona, Spain. Boulmerka has been awarded a Medal of Merit and is a role model for many of her fellow Algerians. She has, however, been the target of death threats from Islamic extremists in Algeria who disapprove of her running attire.

## Other Sports

Algeria has achieved much success in other sports, most notably track and field and boxing. In 2000, Algeria placed thirty-seventh in the medal standings at the Olympics held in Sydney, Australia. The country won a total of five medals, including a gold in the women's 1,500-meter event. Two well-known Algerian athletes are Hassiba Boulmerka and Noureddine Morceli. Both are Olympic gold medal winners in the 1,500-meter event.

In 1996, Hocine Soltani became the first Algerian to win an Olympic gold medal for boxing in the lightweight category. He also received a bronze medal at the 1992 Barcelona Olympics in the featherweight category. Other medal-winning Algerian boxers include Mohammed Zaoul, Mustapha Moussa, and Mohamed Bahari.

In 1934, Algerian Marcel Cerdan (1916–1949) started his professional boxing career. Known as the "Casablanca Clouter," Cerdan was crowned the French champion in 1945. Two years later, he won the title of European champion. In 1962, *Ring* inducted Cerdan into the magazine's Boxing Hall of Fame.

**AN ALGERIAN TRACK STAR**

**Noureddine Morceli was born in 1970, one half of a set of twins. When he was seven, Morceli followed in his older brother's footsteps and began running. Ten years later, he won second place in the world junior championships. In the years that followed, Morceli earned medals in the 1,500-m (indoor and outdoor), the mile, and the 3,000-m events. A devout Muslim, Morceli fasts during Ramadan even when he is training hard. He has been awarded the title of "Athlete of the Year" once by the International Athletic Foundation and twice by *Track & Field News*.**

# Holidays and Festivals

Islamic festivals feature prominently in the Algerian calendar of holidays. The first important festival is Eid al-Seghir, which marks the end of the holy month of Ramadan, the Islamic period of compulsory fasting. Ramadan is the time when Muslims must refrain from physical pleasures, including food and drink, during the day and make extra effort not to have evil thoughts or do bad deeds.

Eid al-Seghir is celebrated over two days. Celebrations begin with prayers at a mosque. Alms are given to the poor and children receive presents and money.

The second important festival is Eid al-Kebir, which occurs in the last month of the Muslim calendar. The feast celebrates Abraham's strong faith and devotion to God, as shown by his willingness to sacrifice his son. On Eid al-Kebir, families offer a sacrificial sheep for slaughter, and the meat is shared among relatives, friends, and the poor.

Other Algerian holidays are related to the country's fight for independence. Revolution Day is a national holiday celebrated on November 1 that marks the start of the Algerian War of Independence. The date is the anniversary of the first guerilla attacks directed at certain facilities that were then controlled and operated by the French. The attacks were organized by the FLN, who then called on all Algerian Muslims to help them in the struggle for nationhood.

July 5 is known in Algeria as Independence Day. The date marks the day when Algeria was granted independence from France. Historical Readjustment Day falls on June 19. This holiday commemorates the day when Ahmed Ben Bella was ousted from power by Houari Boumedienne.

Local Algerian festivals are known as *moussem* (MOO-sem). In the oasis town of Taghit, a festival called Moussem Taghit celebrates the harvesting of dates. During spring, many cities have moussems to celebrate the harvests of various crops. The city of Adrar has a moussem for tomatoes, while Tlemcen has one for cherries.

*Above:* **Moussems are important to the Berber people because these festivals allow the various Berber clans to gather and celebrate. Moussems usually take place near the end of the summer season. The festivities include a dance performed by young Berber girls.**

*Opposite:* **Muslim Berbers begin the feast of Eid al-Kebir by facing the rising sun for communal morning prayers.**

# Food

Algerian cuisine has influences from various cultures. Algerians learned how to include spices in their cooking and to create different types of pastries from the Turks and the Arabs. Algerians are also fond of olives from Spain and breads from France. Around the city of Oran, in the northwestern part of the country, foods such as paella are widespread, showing the strong Spanish influence in this area.

## Typical Algerian Foods

The staple food of Algeria is couscous, which is a fine semolina grain. Couscous is usually steamed and eaten with meat or vegetables and a sauce. Stews, which are common in Berber cooking, are also popular among Algerians. *Tajine* (tah-JEEN) is a stew prepared with lamb or chicken, and *shakshuka* (shak-SHOO-ka) is a stew made of vegetables. *Chorba* (CHOR-ba) is a spicy stew made with herbs, vegetables, and a type of meat, which is usually lamb or chicken.

Another favorite Algerian dish is *burek* (BOO-rek), which is an egg, meat, and onion mixture in phyllo pastry. Other traditional Algerian dishes include charcoal-roasted lamb, spicy lamb sausages, and meat-stuffed vegetables.

## Sweets and Drinks

A wide range of pastries is made in Algeria. Some of these pastries are made with figs and dates, and some are made of semolina, rose water, almond paste, butter, and honey. Pastries filled with almonds and honey are especially popular.

Algerians often like to drink a beverage when they are relaxing and talking with friends. Their favorite beverages include mint-flavored tea and sweet, strong coffee that is served with a glass of water. Fruit-based drinks are also popular.

Before 1962, Algeria had a growing wine industry under the French. Islam, however, does not allow its followers to drink alcohol, and wine production in the country declined when the French left. Today, the Algerian wine industry is facing a revival, and about three-quarters of the wine produced is exported.

*Above:* **Brochettes are kebobs that are served with French bread. Restaurants in the city of Algiers and a number of coastal towns commonly serve French and Italian food. The cuisine at these restaurants, however, tends to be spicier than cuisine served at similar restaurants in Europe.**

*Opposite:* **In Algeria, couscous is prepared by steaming semolina over water and mixing it with melted butter. Northern Algerians prefer to use semolina made from hard wheat. Southern Algerians, however, prefer to use a mixture of soft wheat, barley, and rye.**

# A CLOSER LOOK AT ALGERIA

Algeria is the second largest country on the African continent. The Sahara Desert covers a large part of the country and is the site of unusual rock formations and ancient rock paintings. The Sahara is also the home of the Tuaregs, a nomadic people descended from the original people who used to occupy Algeria.

The country's location along the Mediterranean coast has made Algeria a prime target for colonizers. The Romans set up a number of cities, the ruins of which are still present today. The Turks also conquered Algeria and left traces of their architectural traditions — such as the Kasbah — in the country.

*Opposite:* **The ancient city of Djémila was once a Roman military garrison known as Cuicul. Djémila was made a UNESCO World Heritage site in 1982.**

Before it was granted independence from French rule, the country went through an intense conflict, the events of which have been dramatized in the movie *The Battle of Algiers*. The struggle for self-rule also helped to create the FLN, Algeria's dominant political party.

Algeria is one of the world's top producers of crude oil and natural gas. In the arts, the country has been the homeland of a number of well-known musicians and literary figures. In spite of its many achievements, Algeria's women still face serious oppression.

*Above:* **The fortified city of Ghardaïa is known for its white and red clay buildings. The structures are built on a slope. At its peak is a mosque that resembles a pyramid.**

# The Battle of Algiers

## The Making of the Movie

Saadi Yacef was a former military commander of the Algerian FLN independence movement. In 1964, Yacef approached Italian film director Gillo Pontecorvo about making a film based on his memoirs. The movie would showcase Algeria's struggle for independence from French colonial rule.

After months of negotiation, Pontecorvo agreed to work with Yacef on the project. The Italian collaborated with Franco Solinas on a script, and Yacef's Algeria-based film company coproduced the movie. Pontecorvo directed the film and cast Yacef as an FLN leader. With Yacef's involvement in the movie, the Algerian government agreed to support the film and allowed the production crew to film within the city of Algiers.

In the entire movie, Pontecorvo used only one professional actor — Jean Martin, who played the role of Colonel Mathieu. The remaining cast members were made up of ordinary people Pontecorvo picked off the streets in Algiers. Brahim Haggiag, who portrayed the main character of Ali la Pointe, was actually an illiterate farmer who was discovered at a market.

### THE STORYLINE OF THE MOVIE

The movie focuses on events that happened between 1954 and 1957. The main character is Ali la Pointe, a poor and uneducated resident of the Kasbah who joins the FLN and becomes one of its leaders. Through la Pointe, the director tells the story of how the Algerian independence movement transformed from a small group of activists to a mass uprising that eventually drove the French out of Algeria.

*Left:* At one time, Gillo Pontecorvo intended to produce a film on the Algerian-French war as seen through the eyes of a French paratrooper. He had wanted to shoot the movie in Algeria but was not granted access to certain areas within Algiers. Pontecorvo then decided to shelve the project.

## The Audience's Reaction

In 1965, the film *The Battle of Algiers* was released and made an immediate impact. The black and white movie was so true to life that viewers thought that it was a documentary. Before it, no other film had captured the horrors of war so vividly. Shocked audiences watched scenes of children shooting at soldiers and disguised Arab women planting bombs in cafés. The realism of the movie was enhanced by a message at the start of the movie proclaiming that none of the scenes shown were taken from footage shot for news reports.

Initially, the French government banned the film. Certain scenes were censored in the United States and the United Kingdom. This, however, did not stop the film from being nominated in the Best Foreign Language Film category for the 1966 Academy Awards and the Best Director and Best Screenplay categories at the 1968 Academy Awards. The film also won the Golden Lion at the 1966 Venice Film Festival. In 2004, *The Battle of Algiers* was remastered and released on DVD with the cut scenes restored.

*Above:* **Saadi Yacef was a commander in the FLN who fought in the Algerian war of independence against the French. It was Yaacef who went in search of someone to produce a film based on his experiences.**

# The Berbers Fight Back

## The Berbers

Most Algerians are descended from the Berber people who were the original residents of North Africa. The majority of Berber communities were centered in the desert and mountain regions of Algeria, Egypt, Libya, Morocco, and Tunisia. At the start of the twenty-first century, there were approximately 4.3 million Berbers in Algeria, making up about 13 percent of the population.

In the seventh century, Arabs conquered North Africa and introduced their language, Arabic, and their religion, Islam, to the countries they colonized. The Berbers put up a strong resistance but finally converted to Islam. The ones who claimed Arabic as their main language were welcomed into Arab society. The rest retained many native Berber social customs and dialects. Today, Berbers are separated into groups that are known by the dialects they speak. These include the Beraber, Rif, Kabyle, Haratin, Shawia, Tuareg, and Shluh.

**THE BERBER LANGUAGES**

The Berber group of languages and dialects is part of the group of Afro-Asiatic languages. Its writing system was passed down from ancient Libyan.

*Below:* The word "Berber" comes from the Roman word for barbarian. Modern Berbers are offended by the name and call themselves Amazigh, which comes from their historic name, Maxyes.

# Fighting Back

Since the country gained independence in 1962, the Berbers have disagreed with the Algerian government on a number of issues. One major area of discontent was the government's refusal to make the Berber language an official language of Algeria. The Berbers also complained about high unemployment, the shortage of housing in Berber areas, and the lack of government spending to improve their lives. Underlying all the complaints was a feeling that the Berbers were marginalized by the Algerian authorities, even though they were the country's original inhabitants.

On a number of occasions, the Berbers have protested against government policy and demanded respect for their rights. In 2001, violent clashes between Berber protesters and government forces broke out in the mountainous Kabylie region, east of the city of Algiers. This was sparked off by the death of a Berber youth during questioning by the gendarmerie, the Algerian countryside police. The skirmishes caused the deaths of more than one hundred protesters.

In 2002, the Algerian government finally agreed to recognize Tamazight, the language of the Berbers, as a national language. The government also consented to include Tamazight as one of the languages in the country's education system.

*Above:* **The majority of Berbers are Muslim. Women in Berber society, however, enjoy more personal freedom than Arab women.**

**STUDENT UPRISING**

In 1980, Berber students felt that the Algerian government's policies promoting Arabization were an attempt to suppress the Berber culture and heritage. The students held demonstrations and went on strike.

# Albert Camus

## His Life

Albert Camus was born on November 7, 1913. A year after his birth, his father, a poor agricultural worker, died while fighting in World War I. His illiterate mother moved the family moved to the Belcourt area of Algiers.

While attending primary school, Camus's intelligence drew the attention of Louis Germain, a teacher. Germain helped the boy to gain a scholarship to the *lycée* and later the University of Algiers. Camus was greatly interested in sports, but tuberculosis deprived him of his strength and a career in sports. The disease also made it difficult for him to study. In 1936, Camus graduated with a degree in philosophy.

In the 1930s, Camus was involved in the Workers' Theater where he wrote, acted, produced, and adapted plays targeted at a working-class audience. In 1937, Camus apprenticed with the newspaper *Alger-Républicain*. During World War II, Camus became the editor of *Combat*, a French Resistance newspaper.

### THE FUTILITY OF LIFE

Faced with death from a young age, Camus was always thinking about the meaning of life. His works explored how meaningless life can seem to be. This was the topic of his essay *The Myth of Sisyphus*. In Greek mythology, Sisyphus was a Corinthian king. As a punishment in the afterlife, he had to roll a boulder up a hill. As soon as he reached the top, the huge rock would roll back down the hill. Sisyphus had to repeat this action over and over forever, with no hope of ever getting the boulder to stay at the top of the hill. For Camus, life was as futile as Sisyphus's attempts to make the boulder stay atop the hill.

*Left:* In 1957, Albert Camus was awarded the Nobel Prize for Literature. In his acceptance speech, he dedicated the award to his mentor, Louis Germain. Camus died in a fatal car accident in Paris, France, in 1960.

## His Major Works

Camus was a prolific writer. His early works include a series of essays called *The Wrong Side and the Right Side* (1937). In these essays, he described his youth in Belcourt and his mother, his grandmother, and his uncle. His first novel, *The Stranger*, was published in 1942 and explored the idea of being an outsider in society. In the same year, Camus published a philosophical paper entitled *The Myth of Sisyphus*. His second work on philosophical themes, *The Rebel*, was written about a decade later in 1951.

Camus's second novel, *The Plague*, was released in 1947. This book was followed by *The Fall* (1956) and *Exile and the Kingdom* (1957), a collection of stories.

His great love of the theater led him to write two memorable plays, *Cross Purpose* (1944) and *Caligula* (1945). Camus was also respected for his brilliant stage adaptations of two books: William Faulkner's *Requiem for a Nun* (1956) and Fyodor Dostoyevsky's *The Possessed* (1959).

*Above:* During a drama festival at Angers in France, Camus showed his love for the theater by directing a performance of *Olmedo*, by Lope Félix de Vega Carpio.

# City of Constantine

Situated on top of a plateau that is surrounded by a steep gorge, the city of Constantine is a natural fort. For this reason, different foreign influences have — time and again — attempted to capture the city in the hopes of setting up a base.

## Historical Background

Known as Cirta in ancient times, Constantine was one of the most important cities in North Africa. In the second century B.C., while under Carthaginian rule, the city reached the peak of its wealth. Under Roman rule, Constantine served as the center of four Roman North African colonies. Cirta was later destroyed during a war between the Romans and the North Africans. In A.D. 313, the city was rebuilt by the Roman emperor, Constantine the Great, and renamed in his honor. The city remained under Roman rule until the Arabs of the Ottoman Empire invaded and seized it in the seventh century.

Over the centuries, the Arabs would lose and regain control of Constantine a number of times. The city eventually became the seat of the Ottoman rulers in Algeria. In 1826, Constantine

**THE GORGE**

A deep ravine surrounds the city of Constantine on three sides. The distances between the gorge cliffs range from 15 feet (4.5 m) at the narrowest point to 1,200 feet (365 m) at the widest point.

*Below:* **Constantine was named for the emperor who restored the city after it was destroyed, Constantine the Great. The walls fortifying the city are made of masonry that dates back to Roman times.**

separated itself from the Ottoman Empire and became independent. In 1836, the French attempted to take the city but failed. In 1837, the French tried again and were successful.

## The City Today

Constantine sits on a flat piece of rock 2,130 feet (650 m) above sea level. Virtually cut off from its surroundings except in the southwest, the city can be approached either by the el-Kantara Bridge in the northeast or by the Sidi M'Cid suspension bridge in the north. A viaduct was constructed in the south part of the city, and a river runs through the eastern part of the gorge.

Today, Constantine's industrial sector primarily produces woolen fabrics and leather goods. The city also has a factory that manufactures diesel engines and tractors. Agricultural products, such as grain, are traded mainly on the High Plateau and in the Sahara, which tends to have a drier climate. As of 2004, the population of the city was about 544,000.

In 1969, the University of Constantine was founded. The city is also home to the Municipal Library, the Museum of Cirta, and an international airport.

*Above:* **The Sidi M'Cid suspension bridge is one of the two bridges that links Constantine to the outside world. It is 525 ft (160 m) long and spans a canyon 656 ft (200 m) deep.**

**DIFFERENT INFLUENCES**

**The city is divided into two parts by the Rue Didouche Moutad, and the two sections reflect different cultures. French influence is stronger in the western sector. The southeastern and eastern sector has more Islamic influences. One unique feature of this sector is that each street is devoted to a different craft.**

# The Engine of Algeria's Economy

Oil and natural gas are the backbone of the Algerian economy. In 2002, oil, gas, and related products accounted for 97 percent of the country's exports. About 7 percent of this amount was exported to the United States.

## Oil

In 1956, oil was first discovered at Hassi Messaoud, situated in the northeastern portion of the Algerian Sahara Desert. The oil from Algeria is considered among the highest quality in the world because it lacks many of the impurities, such as sulfur and metals, that are sometimes found in crude oil. Today, Algeria is one of the eleven countries belonging to the Organization of Petroleum Exporting Countries (OPEC). In 2004, it is expected to contribute about 3 percent of OPEC's total quota of oil.

In 1963, Algeria founded the state-owned company called Société Nationale de Transport et de Commercialisation des Hydrocarbures (Sonatrach). It handles all of Algeria's hydrocarbon mining, production, and export activities.

**OPEC COUNTRIES**

Together, the OPEC countries own more than 75 percent of the world's crude oil deposits and produce about 40 percent of the world's total output.

*Below:* **Algeria's crude oil is extracted from three main oil fields. The largest is located at Hassi Messaoud, the site where oil was first discovered in Algeria. The other two are Zarzaïtine-Edjeleh, located along the border with Libya, and El-Borma, located along the border with Tunisia.**

About 90 percent of the crude oil extracted in Algeria is exported to Western Europe, where the primary buyer is Italy. Other countries importing Algeria's oil are Germany, France, the Netherlands, Spain, and the United Kingdom. Algeria's oil is piped directly from the oil fields to the Mediterranean ports, where it is then transported to the various countries.

*Above:* **Men at work in a gas factory. In January 2004, an explosion at a Skikda liquified natural gas (LNG) plant killed twenty-three people and injured seventy-four.**

## Natural Gas

In 1956, natural gas deposits were first discovered at Hassi R'Mel. Since then, Algeria has become the world's second largest exporter of natural gas. The country has the world's fifth largest reserves of natural gas. In 2001, the country helped to found the Gas Exporting Countries' Forum (GECF), a group of nations that collectively possesses about 66 percent of the world's natural gas reserves.

In 2000, Algeria exported about 20 percent of its natural gas to the European Union. By 2001, the country had two pipelines for exporting gas. The Trans-Mediterranean runs from Algeria, through Tunisia and Sicily, to Italy. The Maghrib-Europe line connects the country with Spain and Portugal. A third pipeline, the Medgaz, which was proposed in 2001, will be a direct link to Spain.

### GAS EXPORTING COUNTRIES' FORUM (GECF)

The GECF is now made up of fifteen countries: Algeria, Bolivia, Brunei, Egypt, Indonesia, Iran, Libya, Malaysia, Nigeria, Oman, Qatar, Russia, Venezuela, the United Arab Emirates (UAE), and Trinidad & Tobago. In March 2004, Egypt hosted the forum's Fourth Ministerial Meeting. The meeting was attended by all the member countries except Bolivia. In 2005, Trinidad & Tobago will host the next meeting.

# Feminist Assia Djebar

## Her Life

Originally named Fatima-zohra Imalayan, Assia Djebar was born in Cherchell, a town west of Algiers, in 1936. She was the first Algerian woman accepted into Paris's prestigious École Normale Supérieure. In 1956, during Algeria's initial uprising against the French, Djebar joined other Algerian students to protest on the streets of Paris. Later, she wrote articles for the FLN's newspaper.

After Algeria's independence, Djebar returned home to teach history and pursue her writing. Many Algerians criticized Djebar for continuing to write in French, as opposed to Arabic, which was now the official language of Algeria. Djebar began studying classical Arabic literature, but continued to write in French, the language in which she had been educated. Currently, Djebar is the Silver Chair for French at New York University in New York City.

## Her Works

In 1957, Djebar published her first novel, entitled *The Mischief*. The story is about a young girl of mixed heritage — Algerian and French — who tries to live a Western lifestyle in Algeria. Her second novel, *The Impatient Ones*, appeared a year later. In 1962, Djebar published *Children of the New World*. *The Naive Larks* followed in 1967. Both novels show how feminism in Algeria had gained prominence. The books also highlight the deeds of Algerian women during the country's fight for independence.

In 1969, Djebar and her husband, Walid Garn, wrote and published a play entitled *Red Is the Dawn*. In the same year, she also wrote a collection of poems called *Poems for a Happy Algeria*. In 1978, Djebar produced her first film, *La Nouba des femmes du Mont Chenoua*, a story about a female Algerian engineer who returned to her homeland after a long period of staying in the West. The film won the 1979 International Critics Prize at the Venice Film Festival.

Djebar continued writing novels. In 1980, a collection of short stories titled *Women of Algiers in Their Apartment* was published. This was followed by *Fantasia: An Algerian Cavalcade*, in 1985, and *A Sister to Scheherazade*, in 1987.

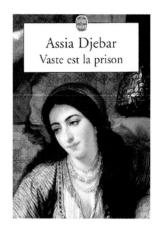

*Above:* In 1995, Djebar published *So Vast the Prison*, a novel that is based on her own life. In the book, she describes life from the perspective of a modern, educated woman in Algeria.

*Opposite:* In 1997, Djebar won the Marguerite Yourcenar Prize for Literature. In 1996, she was honored with the International Literary Neustadt Prize. In 1997, Djebar received the International Prize of Palmi for Creative Work. In 1999, the Belgian Royal Academy of French Language and Literature elected Djebar as a member. The author was also awarded the Peace Prize by the German Association of Book Traders in 2000.

# Front de Libération Nationale (FLN)

## Birth of a Political Party

French domination of Algeria led to the founding of a number of political parties. The parties were eager to break away from French colonial rule. The groups realized that it would not be possible for Algeria to gain independence through peaceful means. In March 1954, a few members of a disbanded military group formed the Comité Révolutionnaire d'Unité et d'Action (CRUA), or the Revolutionary Committee of Unity and Action. CRUA later evolved into the Front de Libération Nationale (FLN), or National Liberation Front. The FLN aimed to bring the various nationalist groups together and mount an armed revolt against the French in order to liberate Algeria.

In 1956, the FLN organized its party structure and divided Algeria into six autonomous zones. Each zone was headed by a district head who reported to the party's executive body.

**INTERNAL WORKING OF THE FLN**

The FLN reworked its party structure so that the organization was similar to a provisional government. The FLN had an executive body that consisted of five people and a legislative body that included all the district heads.

# Fighting for Independence

Algeria's war of independence against the French lasted from 1954 to 1962. The war was characterized by guerrilla tactics, acts of terrorism, and strikes. The French finally agreed to a cease-fire in a treaty signed with the FLN at Évian-les-Bains in France. The treaty was accepted by the Algerian people in a referendum, and Algeria became independent soon after.

Independence, however, triggered a power struggle within the FLN. Some members of the FLN, including Ahmed Ben Bella and Houari Boumedienne, opposed other FLN members and set up the Political Bureau. The Political Bureau proposed a socialist system of government based on Islamic principles and gained a strong following. Popular support for the policies of the Political Bureau allowed Ben Bella to be elected president in 1963. Two years later, Boumedienne ousted Ben Bella in a coup. As president of the country and leader of the FLN, Boumedienne kept a tight control of the government and the party until he died in 1978. From Algeria's independence until 1989, the FLN was the only political party in control of the government.

*Above:* **In August 1955, the FLN launched an armed attack in the town of Skikda. FLN troops killed about one hundred European citizens and Muslim officials. Angry French then retaliated. The assault that followed claimed the lives of thousands of Algerians.**

*Opposite:* **Ahmed Ben Bella (*left*) was one of the founding members of the FLN. Before he was elected president, Ben Bella served the FLN well as a leader, and escaped death twice. In a coup led by his rival, Houari Boumedienne (*right*), Ben Bella was ousted from power.**

# The Jews of Algeria

Since the first century A.D., Jews have been present in Algeria. The first Jews to move to Algeria were from Palestine, which was under Roman rule at the time. The Algerian Jewish community today, however, is not large.

## Immigrants from Spain

In the fourteenth century, conflicts in Spain drove large numbers of Jews to flee and settle in Algeria, which was predominantly Muslim. Despite persecution from the host country, the Jewish community was able to hold its own and grow in quantity.

In 1830, Algeria became a colony of France, and the Algerian Jews gradually began adopting French customs. In 1870, the Cremieux Decree granted all Algerian Jews the right to be French citizens. This was an attempt by the French government to establish itself as a presence in Algeria. Through this action,

*Left:* This stone synagogue in Algiers has been abandoned because the small number of Jews in Algeria are afraid of being targeted by terrorists.

*Above:* **An Algerian Jewish couple from the 1950s.**

the French government was also hoping to win the support of the Algerian Jews and create a rift between the Jews and the Arab majority in the French colony.

In 1934, an uprising in Constantine killed twenty-five Jews and left many more injured. The violence was triggered by the anti-Semitic behavior of the Nazis in Germany. By 1948, the country's Jewish population had grown to 140,000.

## After Algeria's Independence

By the time Algeria gained independence in 1962, about 130,000 members of the Jewish community had fled to France. In 1994, many of the remaining Jews abandoned the last synagogue in Algiers and left the country when faced with threats of violence from terrorists. For security reasons, most Jews who chose to remain in the country live in the city of Algiers. Only a few Jews still live in the cities of Oran and Blida.

Today, Islam is the state religion of Algeria. Algerian law bans public gatherings if the meetings are for the purpose of any religious worship outside of Islam, so the country's Jews resort to meeting in their homes. In 2001, it was estimated that there were less than one hundred Jews in Algeria.

# The Kasbah of Algiers

Algiers is the administrative capital of Algeria and the largest city in the country. Nestled on a steep hill within the city is the Kasbah, which was designated a UNESCO World Heritage site in 1992.

## Why It Was Chosen

The Kasbah of Algiers is a medina that showcases the historical, architectural, and cultural traditions of the precolonial rulers that inhabited Algeria. Triangular in shape, the section is situated just before the citadel that stands at the top of the hill. Looking out over the Mediterranean Sea, the Kasbah was constructed on a slope about 387 feet (118 m) above sea level.

The architecture of the Kasbah is a combination of Moorish, Turkish, and Arab-Mediterranean elements. Some of the major landmarks in the section include the Great Mosque, the Dar Aziz Bent El Rey Palace, the Sidi Abd-al-Rahman Mosque, and the Ketchaoua Mosque. Sculpted wood and earthenware can be found at a number of these monuments, which also have gardens and fountains within their compounds.

*Above:* **Flat-topped buildings with high, whitewashed walls are a common feature of the Algerian Kasbah. The walls line both sides of the passageways and make the Kasbah like a maze.**

## Life in the Kasbah

In the late 1990s, the Kasbah was a crowded and dangerous place. Home to more than 70,000 people, the Kasbah was overcrowded. It was common to find thirty to forty people living in the same house, with few rooms to share between them. Much of the crime in the city of Algiers stemmed from criminals who lived in dilapidated houses within the Kasbah. In addition, debris from demolished Kasbah buildings littered the streets and made it difficult and unsafe for people to move around. Terrorist attacks in the area had also made the people fear for their lives.

By 1999, the authorities had taken steps to change the situation. A plan was put in place to reduce the number of people living in the Kasbah so that it would not be so crowded. Police stations were set up to keep the peace and make the citizens feel safe again. The debris in the streets was also cleared to improve sanitary conditions. Conservation plans were put in place to restore the Kasbah and the city of Algiers to their former glory.

*Opposite:* **In Algeria's Kasbah, a tight network of narrow, winding passageways are cut by stairs that follow the gradient of the hill.**

# The Legacy of Rome

## Roman Rule of North Africa

The Romans ruled North Africa for more than five hundred years. In that time, they established a number of Roman cities, many of which were in Algeria. Most of these cities grew properous from agriculture. By the first century A.D., Roman-ruled North Africa was producing one million tons of grain annually and exporting 25 percent of this amount. These exports fulfilled two-thirds of Roman grain needs. Not surprisingly, North Africa soon became known as the "granary of the empire." By the following century, olive oil was another important North-African export.

## Roman Ruins in Algeria

In A.D. 100, the ancient Roman city of Thamugadi was founded by Emperor Trajan (A.D. 53–117) for military purposes. Currently known as Timgad, the extensive site is one of North Africa's best preserved Roman ruins. Located north of the Aurés Mountains on a high plateau, the ruins show evidence of a town that was well planned and comfortable for those living in it. The remains

**ROMAN EMPERORS**

The Roman cities in North Africa were founded by three different emperors. Claudius (10 B.C.–A.D. 54) established Tingis, Caesarea, and Tipasa. Thamugadi and various cities north of the Aurés Mountains were founded by Trajan. Nerva (A.D. 30–98) established the cities of Cuicul and Sitifis.

*Below:* **A museum was set up near the entrance to the Djémila ruins in order to preserve the magnificent mosaics that were excavated at the site.**

point to the existence of numerous public baths, a public library, a forum, and a theater that seated an audience of 4,000. The streets were constructed at right-angled intersections, in the style typical of classic Roman cities. In the sixth century, invading Berbers captured and plundered the city.

Another well preserved site of Roman ruins is the city of Djémila. Originally known as Cuicul, the remains of this ancient city show evidence of excellent Roman town planning. The plan of this town was designed to suit its mountainous location. Djémila is located about 2,950 ft (900 m) above sea level and was founded as a military garrison by the Roman emperor Nerva. The city was abandoned in the fifth century but the ruins show that it once had two forums, two basilicas, a temple, a baptistry, and an arch. Evidence of a 3,000-seat theater also exists, although this was located outside the city walls. A Roman bath, with its pipes and double panels for the circulation of hot water, can still be seen today.

*Above:* **Originally a Phoenician trading center, the ancient coastal city of Tipasa was captured by the Romans in the second century A.D. but was destroyed in the fifth century. Currently, a modern village stands near the ancient ruins. Founded in 1857, the village is also called Tipasa.**

### UNESCO WORLD HERITAGE SITES

**In 1982, Timgad, Djémila, and Tipasa were declared UNESCO World Heritage sites.**

# Rai Music

## Origins of Rai Music

The word *rai* comes from the Arabic word *ra'y* (RAH-ee), which means "advice" or "opinion." Rai music is based on a form of sung poetry called *malhun* (mal-HOON), which was usually performed by male poets known as *cheikhs* (SHAKES).

During the 1920s, the seaport of Oran had many taverns which were visited by the foreign troops stationed in the city. A number of women, known as *cheikhas* (SHAKE-has), supported themselves by entertaining the troops with songs and dances. This was the start of rai music.

Over the years, rai incorporated influences from Egyptian and Moroccan music, Western rock, and Jamaican reggae. The traditional instruments used during the early days of rai are now complemented by electric guitars, synthesizers, and drums. One characteristic of rai music that has not changed is that it is upbeat and danceable.

The lyrics of rai music speak of everyday life and cover topics like alienation, poverty, suffering, and even drug abuse. Not surprisingly, rai became popular among the urban youth and others members of society who felt ignored or left out. After the country's independence in 1962, the government

*Below:* In 2001, the district of Bab el-Oued in the city of Algiers was badly damaged by a flood. The calamity destroyed buildings and killed people. In November 2001, a charity concert was held in Paris, France. The funds raised during the concert went toward helping the victims of Bab el Oued rebuild their lives and homes. Cheb Khaled and his wife, Samira (*left*), were present at the concert.

*Left:* **Khelifati Muhammad was once a welder like his father. He began singing at the age of twelve. He records under the name of Cheb Mami, which means "the young mourner" in Arabic.**

banned rai because the music was considered disruptive to society. In the mid-1980s, however, radio stations in southern France began playing rai, and the Algerian government's suppression of the music failed.

## Rai Singers

Male singers of rai are known as *cheb* (SHABB), and many modern rai singers add this term to their names. One of the most famous is Cheb Khaled, who is known as the "king of rai" to most Algerians. Born Khaled Hadj Brahim in 1960, Khaled was a talented boy who played a number of musical instruments by the age of ten. He recorded his first single at fourteen. In 1985, Algeria hosted the first international rai festival, with Khaled as the featured performer. In 1990, Khaled fled to France after receiving death threats from Islamic extremists who were offended by his music and lifestyle. Khaled has not returned to his homeland since then.

Another famous rai singer is Cheb Mami. Known as the "prince of rai," Mami was born Khelifati Muhammad in 1966. In 1982, he was spotted by record producers after coming in second in a talent competition on the radio. In 1999, the world came to know Cheb Mami through the song "Desert Rose," on which Mami collaborated with British singer Sting.

# Saint Augustine of Hippo

## Early Life

Augustine was born in A.D. 354 in the Algerian town of Tagaste, at a time when Algeria was part of the Roman Empire. Although his mother was a devout Christian, Augustine's father was baptized only on his deathbed. Although Augustine's parents were not very wealthy, the family was respectable, and they made sure that their son received a good education based on classical teachings. Augustine eventually attended a university in Carthage.

After working as a teacher in Carthage for several years, Augustine moved to Rome in 383. Before long, he was appointed imperial professor of rhetoric at Milan, but his career did not take off. After two years, Augustine resigned and returned home. In 387, Augustine agreed to be baptized as a Christian.

**RENAMED TOWNS**

Today, Tagaste is known as Souk Ahras. The town of Hippo is now Annaba.

*Below:* Saint Augustine was Algerian by birth but his influence is so far-reaching that Catholic churches around the world feature statues of him. One such statue stands in the west front of Salisury Cathedral in Wiltshire, United Kingdom.

# Writing for God

In A.D. 396, Augustine was appointed bishop of Hippo, a trading town north of Tagaste. From then until the time of his death in A.D. 430, Augustine served the community in this capacity, teaching people about Christianity. Augustine was a gifted preacher who was able to reach out to the people. His fame, however, came from his writings. Augustine wrote numerous works, many of which still are read today. In his writings, Augustine adapted classical ideas based on the thought of Greek philosophers such as Plato to Christian doctrines.

Two of his greatest and most important works were *Confessions* (397) and *City of God* (412). Written when Augustine was in his early 40s, *Confessions* is a thirteen-chapter work that is based heavily on his own life. Using a middle-aged man as a central character, Augustine writes about the meaning of life, redemption, and how the man accepts his own imperfections.

Augustine's *City of God* spans twenty-two chapters. In this work, Augustine writes about the society in which humans live. In his writings, he encourages readers to accept disappointment, disaster, and death as a part of life, and prepare for the afterlife.

*Above:* **A woodcut showing Augustine speaking to the congregation at Hippo.**

## CONFERENCE ON ST. AUGUSTINE

In 2001, the Algerian government, together with the Higher Islamic Council of Algeria, sponsored a conference in Algiers called "Augustine in Algeria." Augustinian scholars from around the world were invited to participate. President Bouteflika gave the opening address.

# The Status and Rights of Women

## Laws Governing Women

Three sets of laws govern the lives of Algerian women. The Family Code, which was passed in 1984 and is based on Islamic law, governs the personal status of women in Algeria. Under the code, a woman is considered a minor, and her husband or a male relative is considered her legal guardian.

According to the code, a woman must seek the permission of her guardian in order to get married. Women are not allowed to marry non-Muslim men, but the men can marry outside their faith. The code also allows men to take more than one wife. It is difficult for a woman to divorce her husband unless the husband is convicted of a major crime or abandons her. A mother will be given custody of the children, but the father's permission is needed before she is allowed to enroll the children in new schools or take them out of the country. If her husband dies, a woman inherits a smaller portion of his property than her sons or her brothers-in-law claim.

The country's civil and criminal laws, on the other hand, gives Algerian women many of the same rights as men. The civil law allows them to vote, buy, sell and own property, work

**AGAINST THE FRENCH**

While Algeria was under colonial rule, the French wanted to improve the status of women. The French planned better educational opportunities for Algerian women and wanted them to do away with the wearing of veils. Many Algerians thought that this was the French's attempt to gain support from the women. After independence, the Algerian government reverted to traditional Islamic ways.

*Below:* In the city of Ghardaïa, veiled women gather at the front of a carpet shop.

and engage in business, and sign contracts. Under criminal law, women are treated in the same way as men, although they receive lighter punishment in some cases.

## Modern Women

Although civil laws provide some equal rights for Algerian women, in reality, Algerian women are treated unfairly because of the Family Code. The restrictive nature of the Family Code, however, has not stopped women from fighting for their rights. In the early 1980s, a number of women's groups sprung up in Algeria. The groups, which were intent on winning equal rights for Algerian women, included the Committee for the Legal Equality of Men and Women and the Algerian Association for the Emancipation of Women. The number of women who took part in these groups, however, was small. Many women stayed away because they were afraid that the government would retaliate and that the public would look down on them.

Although the Muslim clergy in Algeria were against more freedom for Algerian women, the government was open to the idea of having more women participating in public life. In 1984, the first female cabinet minister was appointed to the Algerian government. By 1997, the National Assembly had eleven elected women. In the 2002 elections, the number of female members in Algeria's parliament doubled from twelve to twenty-four.

**UNION NATIONALE DES FEMMES ALGÉRIENNES (UNFA)**

Women who played a significant part in the war of independence went back to their traditional roles once the conflict was over. In 1962, the government founded a women's society known as the Union Nationale des Femmes Algériennes (UNFA), or the National Union of Algerian Women. In 1965, UNFA celebrated International Women's Day by organizing a march in which 6,000 women took part.

# Tassili n'Ajjer

The vast Sahara Desert covers about four-fifths of Algeria. In the southeastern part of the Algerian Sahara, near the country's borders with Libya and Niger, is a plateau known as Tassili n'Ajjer.

## Geological Formations

Consisting of a series of cliffs, the Tassili, or sandstone plateau, has a unique landscape. The existing land forms are a result of many centuries of climatic change that have swept through this region. Valleys with steep sides were formed by alternating wet and dry climates. In the past, rivers flowed through the plateau into lakes. The rivers, however, have since dried up, leaving behind dry beds and deep gorges, and the lakes have since been transformed into the sand seas known as ergs. The arid environment and erosion by wind created the rock formations, known as "stone forests," that are scattered about the plateau.

*Below:* **The gigantic stone formations that exist at Tassili n'Ajjer are believed to be sculptures that mark tombs.**

## Rock Paintings

The most outstanding features of Tassili n'Ajjer are the prehistoric rock paintings that were discovered in the nineteenth century. More than 15,000 paintings and engravings cover the sides of the plateau. Archaeologists have not been able to accurately date each one. The drawings depict humans and scenes from civilization during the time span from between 6000 B.C. and the first century A.D.

The paintings and engravings of Tassili n'Ajjer fall loosely into four periods. Drawings from the Bubalus period (6000 B.C. – 4500 B.C.) depict wild animals, such as buffalo, and humans with round heads or masks. The appearance of domestic cattle heralds the Cattle period (4500 B.C. – 1200 B.C.) and show humans as herders. Engravings from this period tend to be stiff, but the paintings are more natural. Drawings of horses, chariots, and hunting scenes appeared during the Horse period (1200 B.C. – 700 B.C.). Humans are seen with spears and shields. The Camel period (700 B.C. – A.D. 1) coincides with a time when the area was becoming drier and horses were not used as frequently. The animals depicted here, such as the camel, are similar to those that live in the region today.

*Above:* **This rock painting at Tassili n'Ajjer depicts hunters and humped animals and dates back to the Camel period.**

### ACCESS TO THE SITE

**Tassili n'Ajjer is popular with tourists. The Algerian government has constructed an international airport near Tassili n'Ajjer to make it easier for both tourists and scientists to visit the site.**

# The Tuaregs

Living in parts of the Algerian Sahara Desert, the Tuaregs are a nomadic people who are descended from the Berbers. The Tuaregs speak a Berber dialect known as Tamashek and write in Tifinagh, a script preserved from the time of the ancient Libyans.

## Tuareg Way of Life

One distinctive feature of the Tuaregs is the dark blue or indigo turbans that male Tuaregs wear to cover their heads and faces leaving only the eyes and nose visible. The purpose of this headwear is to keep sand out of the throat and lungs, especially during rides in the desert. This has led Tuaregs be called "the Blue Men." Among Tuareg males, the practice of covering the face in the presence of women, their in-laws, and foreigners, is also a sign of respect.

Being nomads, Tuaregs live in small groups. Each group forms camps consisting of portable tents made from tanned skins that are dyed red. In the past, Tuaregs relied on the raiding of caravans and the robbing of travelers for their livelihoods.

*Below:* Tuaregs are also found in parts of Libya, Mali, and northern Nigeria. The Tuaregs of Algeria are considered the "northern Tuaregs," and they live primarily in the desert area.

Today, however, Tuaregs raise livestock and grow crops, such as wheat and barley. They consider milk a staple food, and they only eat meat during special occasions.

Most Tuaregs are Muslim. Women, however, play a strong role in Tuareg culture, and Tuareg ancestry is traced through the mother's line.

*Above:* **To the Arabs, the Tuaregs are known as "the People of the Veil." Tuareg warriors carry weapons such as double-edged swords, daggers, and lances.**

## Social Structure

Within the Tuareg tribe, there exists a hierarchical structure of five classes. Nobles are the most influential and the chief of a tribe belongs to this class. The position of chief is hereditary and matrilineal. The clergy form the second group. Forming the third class are the serfs who are vassals to the nobles and who are born into this class.

An exception occurs when a child's father is a noble and mother is a serf. Children of this type of union are known as crossbreeds and make up a fourth class within the Tuareg social organization. The fifth class consists of slaves, most of whom are from Sudan. Serfs, crossbreeds, and slaves do almost all of the domestic and manual labor in the tribe.

**TUAREG POLITICS**

The Tuaregs of North Africa fall into five main tribes that are distinguished by where they live. Each tribe is ruled by a chief and an assembly consisting of male members. While the position of chief is usually inherited, the male members of the assembly are usually elected to their positions.

# RELATIONS WITH NORTH AMERICA

The United States and Algeria have a long history of interaction — although it has not always been friendly. In fact, the first contact between Algeria and the newly-independent United States was a military confrontation in the Mediterranean in the nineteenth century. In 1962, when Algeria became independent, both the United States and Canada were quick to recognize the new nation. Unfortunately, the Cold War between the United States and the Soviet Union and the Arab-Israeli conflict, over which the United States and Algeria held opposing positions, caused relations to be tense until the 1980s.

*Opposite:* **American actress Debra Winger on location in the Algerian desert during the filming of the 1990 movie *The Sheltering Sky*. The movie is based on the 1949 novel of the same name by author Paul Bowles.**

Since the end of the Cold War, the United States and Algeria have grown closer. In 2001, Algeria's President Bouteflika became the first Algerian head of state to visit the White House in sixteen years. Both the United States and Canada have tried to bring about a return to peace and stability in Algeria. U.S. and Canadian companies also have been eager to participate in Algeria's oil and gas industry. With the United States, Canada, and Algeria all committed to improving relations, trade and economic cooperation between the nations are likely to increase.

*Above:* **In December 2003, U.S. secretary of state Colin Powell (*left*) met with Algerian foreign minister Abdelaziz Belkhadem in Algiers during the last stage of Powell's three-nation North African tour.**

# Early Relations

When the United States declared its independence from Britain in 1776, U.S. merchant ships in the Mediterranean no longer were protected by the British navy or included in British tribute payments. American ships became the prey of Algerian privateers. In 1794, the United States Congress ordered the construction of warships to protect U.S. ships in the Mediterranean from privateers. In 1797, to avoid conflict, the United States also signed a treaty with the dey of Algiers, the governor of Algeria, that granted the dey U.S. $10 million in tribute in return for assurance that U.S. ships would be safe from privateers for twelve years. This was a lot of money at the time. The tribute to the dey of Algiers accounted for 20 percent of the United States budget in 1800.

In 1815, frustrated by continued privateer attacks, the United States took military action. Commodore Stephen Decatur was sent to the Mediterranean with ten warships to protect U.S. merchant ships and to end the payment of tribute. Decatur captured several privateer ships and sailed into Algiers harbor, threatening to bombard the city with his ships' guns. The dey agreed to stop demanding tribute and to halt attacks against U.S. ships in the Mediterranean. When Decatur left, however, the dey rejected the agreement. In 1816, the reign of the privateers finally came to an end following a combined British and Dutch naval assault on Algiers.

*Left:* **This drawing from the early nineteenth century shows Commodore Decatur of the United States meeting with the dey of Algiers.**

*Left:* **In 1942, during World War II, U.S. soldiers captured Algeria from the French.**

## The French Occupation and World War II

During the French occupation of Algeria, all U.S. commercial relations and other interactions with Algeria were conducted through the French. During World War II, Algeria was initially under control of France's Vichy government. This government had been installed by Nazi Germany after the Germans invaded and occupied France, and it was composed of French officials who either supported or collaborated with Germany. On November 8, 1942, the U.S. army, under the leadership of General Dwight D. Eisenhower, invaded Algeria. The French offered little resistance and surrendered on November 11. For the rest of World War II, Algeria was under the control of the Allies. After the end of the war and Germany's defeat, the new French government resumed its colonial administration over Algeria.

# Independent Algeria and the United States

The United States remained neutral during Algeria's war of independence against France. Most U.S. leaders supported France because they feared that an independent Algeria might fall under the influence of the Soviet Union. One notable exception to this position was Senator John F. Kennedy who, in 1957, urged the U.S. Congress to recognize Algeria's quest for independence. Kennedy's position angered France. Algerians, however, remember his support during their independence struggle.

By 1962, when Algeria declared its independence, Kennedy had become president of the United States, and he sent an ambassador to Algiers. But the warm feelings did not last long. Algeria established a socialist economy that discouraged U.S. investment. Algeria was an outspoken critic of Israel, a close ally of the United States in the Middle East. When Israel launched a preemptive attack against its Arab neighbors in June 1967, Algeria broke off diplomatic relations with the United States to protest the close U.S. relationship with Israel.

In the late 1970s, the United States and Algeria quietly reestablished diplomatic ties. In 1981, Algerian diplomats played a key role in securing the release of fifty-two Americans who were being held hostage by the radical Islamic government

*Below:* **Americans line both sides of Pennsylvania Avenue in Washington, D.C., to cheer the return of the American former hostages of Iran. The release of the hostages after 444 days was secured with the help of the Algerian government.**

*Left:* **On July 12, 2001, Algerian President Abdelaziz Bouteflika (*left*) visited U.S. President George W. Bush (*right*) in the White House. During the visit, the two leaders discussed issues relating to North Africa and the Middle East.**

in Iran. After this incident, the relationship between the United States and Algeria began to improve. Algeria also opened up its economy and slowly abandoned its socialist policies. Algerians sought U.S. investment in its industries. U.S. companies were eager to help develop Algeria's oil and gas sector and to sell their products in Algeria.

In 1992, civil war broke out in Algeria. The United States supported the Algerian government in its fight against the Islamic extremist groups. Many American companies and citizens left Algeria to avoid the violence.

## An Improvement in Relations

In 2000, the violence in Algeria started to diminish and U.S. companies returned to the country. In July 2001, President Bouteflika became the first Algerian president to visit the White House in sixteen years. Algeria publicly condemned the September 11, 2001, terrorist attacks in the United States, and U.S. and Algerian law enforcement officials cooperated on counterterrorism intelligence. Presidents Bush and Bouteflika met again in November 2001 and September 2003. With both the United States and Algeria committed to fighting terrorism and Islamic extremism, the two countries established a new level of friendship and cooperation.

# U.S.-Algerian Trade Relations

In 2002, U.S. direct investment in Algeria totaled U.S. $2.5 billion, most of which was in the oil and gas industries. U.S. companies, however, have also invested in industries such as banking, pharmaceuticals, medical facilities, telecommunications, aviation, and information technology in Algeria. In 2002, a United States chamber of commerce was established in Algiers to encourage further U.S. involvement in Algeria.

Algeria has developed into an important U.S. trade partner, although the United States imports far more from Algeria than it exports to Algeria. In 2003, the U.S. exported U.S. $487.4 million worth of goods to Algeria, while its imports from Algeria were valued at U.S. $4.7 billion. In July 2001, the United States and Algeria signed a trade and investment agreement to facilitate commerce between the two countries.

The United States has offered aid to enable Algeria to rebuild its war-shattered country. The U.S. Department of Agriculture has provided Algeria with grants worth U.S. $50 million for the purchase of U.S. agricultural products, and Algerian military officers receive training in the United States. In June 2003, the United States provided humanitarian aid to Algeria following a massive earthquake in the country. Items such as tents, sleeping bags, water purification equipment, medical kits, and portable kitchens were flown in to help the victims of the quake.

## HUMAN RIGHTS ISSUES

International agencies such as Amnesty International and the Human Rights Watch are keeping a close watch on Algeria. The Algerian government controls all media and limits citizens' freedom of expression. Present laws also discriminate against Berbers and women. Mass graves believed to contain the bodies of civilians who were killed by the military were recently found in the western province of Relizanein. In light of this discovery, human rights organizations have called for countries to ask for greater liberty and equality for the Algerian people in return for economic aid and investment in the country.

*Left:* Algeria is a key trading partner in Africa for the United States. Although the bulk of trade consists of the export of petroleum products from Algeria and the import of essential food and agricultural produce from the United States, U.S. products such as Coca-Cola are also now available all over Algeria.

*Left:* **President Abdelaziz Bouteflika of Algeria rides in an open carriage with a pair of mounties during his five-day visit to Canada in May 2000.**

# Canadian-Algerian Relations

Canada has recognized Algeria's independence since 1962, when it appointed a nonresident ambassador to the country. Christian Hardy became the first resident ambassador to Algeria when the Canadian embassy in Algiers was set up in 1971. Canadian-Algerian relations have been consistently good for over fifty years. In 2000, Algerian president Abdelaziz Bouteflika visited Canada. He told a Canadian audience that Algeria will never forget Canada's understanding during the years that Canada supported the Algerian government during the country's civil war.

Today, Algeria is Canada's largest trading partner in Africa and the Middle East. In 2001, Canada exported CAN $297,028 worth of goods, such as wheat, legumes, newsprint, and milk, to Algeria. In return, Canada imported CAN $1.1 million worth of Algerian goods the same year. Canada's main imports from Algeria are petroleum, dates, figs, and wine.

Canada also provides economic aid to Algeria. It has given Algeria over CAN $150 million since 1964. The money is used to develop programs to improve trade ties, train the Algerian people, and create jobs for them.

# Algerian Immigration to North America

Historically, most Algerian immigration has been to Europe, but thousands of Algerians also have immigrated to Canada. Around 40,000 Algerians live in Canada, mostly in the French-speaking province of Quebec. Some of these immigrants are students who attend Canadian universities. Others have immigrated in search of jobs. Most Algerian immigrants to Canada arrived after 1992, having fled from the civil war. Many Algerian immigrants have not returned home because of unstable political and security conditions in Algeria, leading to the establishment of large Algerian communities in cities such as Montreal.

A smaller number of Algerians has immigrated to the United States. The largest Algerian-American communities are located in Washington, D.C., Houston, Texas, and in cities in northern California. All these areas have associations of Algerian-Americans that help to keep the community cohesive. These associations work to promote better understanding between North Americans and Algerians, to assist Algerian immigrants and students adjust to life in a new country, and to raise money among the Algerian community to help improve the lives of people in Algeria.

Many Algerians living in the United States are professionals. One Algerian immigrant who has succeeded in the United States is Dr. Elias Zerhouni. In 1975, at the age of 24, Zerhouni came to the United States — with little money and a limited knowledge of English — to start work as a radiology resident at the Johns Hopkins University School of Medicine. Over the years, he rose through the ranks at Johns Hopkins. In 2002, United States president George W. Bush nominated him as director of the National Institutes of Health.

After the terrorist attacks in the United States on September 11, 2001, a number of Algerians in both the United States and Canada came under suspicion for supporting terrorist groups. Several Algerians in Canada were deported back to Algeria, and a group of Algerians attempting to cross the border from Canada to the United States was arrested when they were found to be carrying weapons. Nevertheless, the overwhelming majority of Algerians in both the United States and Canada have immigrated to improve their lives and to give their children better opportunities.

*Right:* Algerian-born Dr. Elias Zerhouni (*left*) is congratulated by U.S. president George W. Bush (*right*). Dr. Zerhouni, who was executive vice dean of the Johns Hopkins University School of Medicine, had just been appointed by the president as director of the National Institutes of Health.

## Movies and Music

The beauty of Algeria has captivated some filmmakers. Algeria was one of the locations where award-winning director Bernardo Bertolucci chose to shoot *The Sheltering Sky*. The movie, starring John Malkovich and Debra Winger, so fascinated audiences that the 1949 novel on which it was based made it to the bestseller list.

Algerian rai star Cheb Mami has also earned international fame. Mami, who in 1989 was the first rai musician to visit the United States, gained a greater following after his collaboration with British pop singer Sting on the duet "Desert Rose." The song topped record charts all around the world in 2000.

## Tourism

Because of Algeria's recent civil war, only the most adventurous North Americans have traveled to the country as tourists. Even diplomats and journalists have been reluctant to visit Algeria during periods of extreme violence. The country's oil and gas industry is located mostly in the Sahara Desert, so executives from U.S. and Canadian energy companies have been able to work in Algeria. They have generally avoided traveling to the cities in Algeria's north.

*Above:* **Pop singer Sting (*left*) and Algerian rai star Cheb Mami (*right*) answer questions at a press conference held in Tunis, Tunisia, in April 2001.**

# The Algeria Project

Founded in 1969 in the state of Massachusetts by a group of university students, the Sabre Foundation is an organization that supports education, private-sector growth, and higher learning in developing nations. Its projects have benefitted countries in Africa, the former Soviet Union, the Balkans, Latin America, and the Caribbean.

One of the key projects of the foundation is the Book Donation Program, which started in 1986 to provide new books and educational materials to libraries and schools. Sabre Foundation also conducts training workshops on how to effectively use information technology resources.

Sabre Foundation's Algeria Project took place between 2000 and 2002 and was aided by the then U.S. ambassador to Algeria, Cameron Hume. In phase one of the program, a group of four Algerian librarians were flown to Cambridge, Massachusetts, for a two-week training course on information technology. In November 2002, the second phase of the project took place when 8,060 books, with a value of U.S. $362,198, were shipped to seven universities in northern Algeria. The foundation has since proposed a second shipment of books to universities in Algeria's south. The organization hopes that this will also aid students from Mauritania, Mali, and Niger, some of whom attend universities in southern Algeria.

*Left:* In June 2003, the U.S. ambassador to Algeria Janet Sanderson (*far left*) hosted a reception to honor the work of the Sabre Foundation in Algeria. This picture shows Ambassador Sanderson and a few of the guests attending the reception.

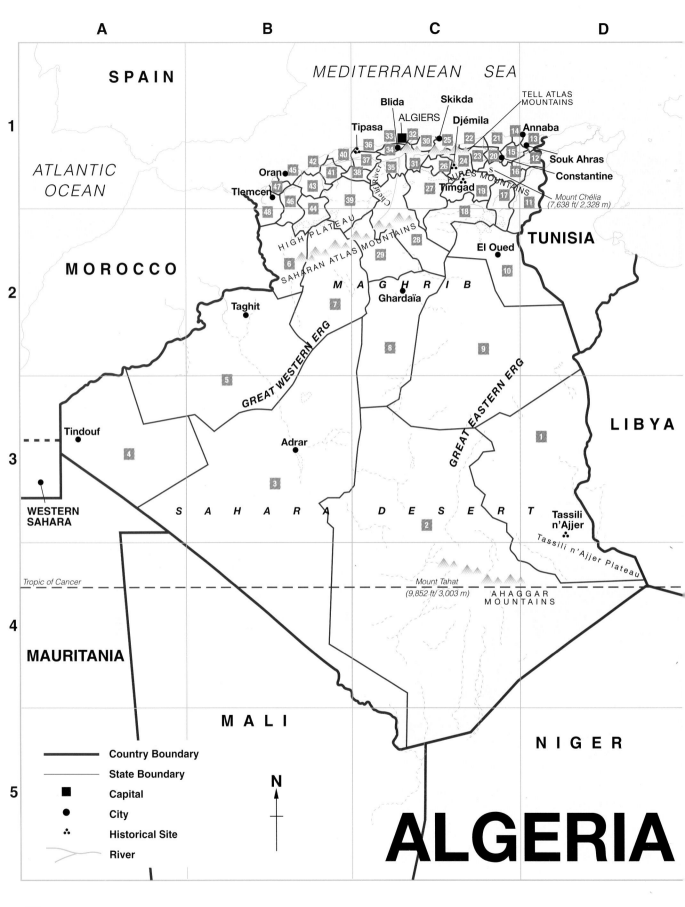

**A**      **B**      **C**      **D**

SPAIN

*MEDITERRANEAN SEA*

TELL ATLAS
MOUNTAINS

Blida   Skikda

Tipasa   ALGIERS   Djémila   Annaba

**1**

*ATLANTIC
OCEAN*

Oran

Tlemcen

Souk Ahras

Constantine

*Mount Chélia
(7,638 ft/ 2,328 m)*

**TUNISIA**

**MOROCCO**

HIGH PLATEAU

Chelif River

SAHARAN ATLAS MOUNTAINS

AURES MOUNTAINS

Timgad

El Oued

*M A G H R I B*

**2**

Taghit

Ghardaïa

GREAT WESTERN ERG

GREAT EASTERN ERG

**L I B Y A**

Tindouf

Adrar

**3**

**WESTERN
SAHARA**

*S A H A R A   D E S E R T*

Tassili
n'Ajjer

*Tassili n'Ajjer Plateau*

*Tropic of Cancer*

*Mount Tahat
(9,852 ft/ 3,003 m)*

A H A G G A R
MOUNTAINS

**4**

**MAURITANIA**

**M A L I**

**N I G E R**

**5**

⸺ Country Boundary

⸺ State Boundary

■ Capital

● City

⸫ Historical Site

～ River

**N**

# ALGERIA

86

*Above:* A man sells his colorful Algerian carpets in the marketplace.

Adrar B3
Ahaggar Mountains C4–D4
Algiers C1
Annaba D1
Aurès Mountains C1

Blida C1

Chelif River B1-C2
Constantine C1

Djémila C1

El Oued C2

Ghardaïa C2
Great Eastern Erg C2–C4, D2–D4
Great Western Erg A3, B2–B4

High Plateau B2–C2

Libya D2–D3

Mali A4–B5
Mediterranean Sea B2-D2

Morocco A3–B2
Mount Chélia C1
Mount Tahat C4

Niger D4–C5
North Atlantic Ocean A1–A2

Oran B1

Sahara Desert B2–D4
Saharan Atlas Mountains B2–C2
Skikda (city) C1
Souk Ahras (city) D1

Spain A1–B1

Taghit B2
Tassili n'Ajjer D3
Tassili n'Ajjer Plateau C3–D4
Tell Atlas Mountains B2-C1
Timgad C1
Tindouf (city) A3
Tipasa C1
Tlemcen B1
Tunisia D1–D2

Western Sahara A3

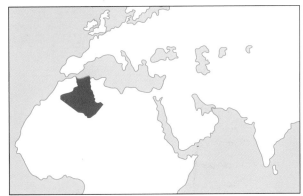

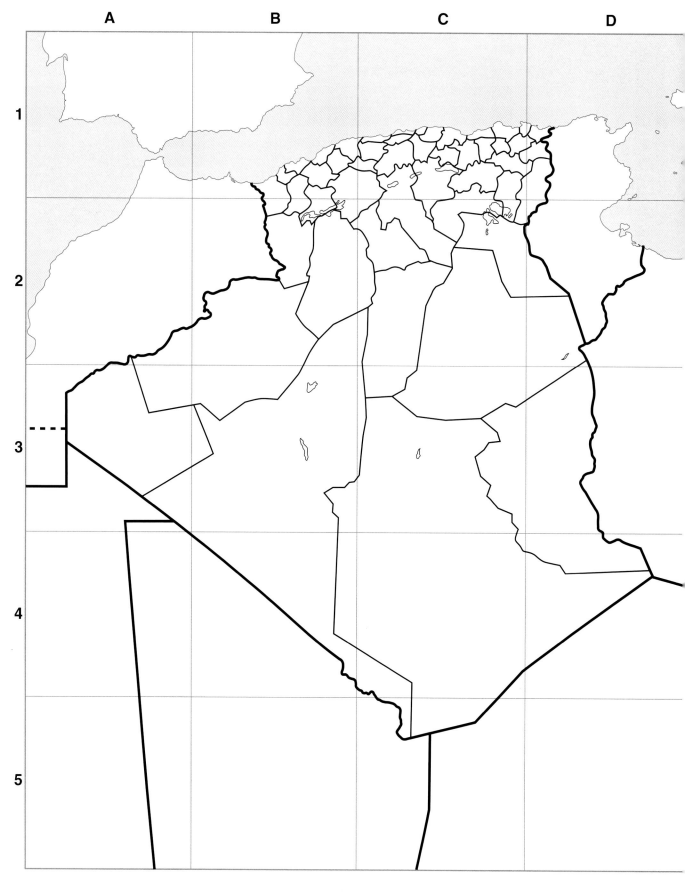

# How Is Your Geography?

Learning to identify the main geographical areas and points of a country can be challenging. Although it may seem difficult at first to memorize the locations and spellings of major cities or the names of mountain ranges, rivers, deserts, lakes, and other prominent physical features, the end result of this effort can be very rewarding. Places you previously did not know existed will suddenly come to life when referred to in world news, whether in newspapers, television reports, other books and reference sources, or on the Internet. This knowledge will make you feel a bit closer to the rest of the world, with its fascinating variety of cultures and physical geography.

This map can be duplicated for use in a classroom. (PLEASE DO NOT WRITE IN THIS BOOK!) Students can then fill in any requested information on their individual map copies. The student can also make a copy of the map and use it as a study tool to practice identifying place names and geographical features on his or her own.

*Below:* **Camels are the main mode of transport for the Tuaregs who live in the Sahara Desert.**

# Algeria at a Glance

**Official Name**     People's Democratic Republic of Algeria

**Capital**     Algiers

**Land Area**     919,595 square miles (2,381,740 square km)

**Administrative Divisions**     Adrar, Ain Defla, Ain Temouchent, Alger, Annaba, Batna, Bechar, Bejaia, Biskra, Blida, Bordj Bou Arreridj, Bouira, Boumerdes, Chlef, Constantine, Djelfa, El Bayadh, El Oued, El Tarf, Ghardaia, Guelma, Illizi, Jijel, Khenchela, Laghouat, Mascara, Medea, Mila, Mostaganem, M'Sila, Naama, Oran, Ouargla, Oum el Bouaghi, Relizane, Saida, Setif, Sidi Bel Abbes, Skikda, Souk Ahras, Tamanghasset, Tebessa, Tiaret, Tindouf, Tipaza, Tissemsilt, Tizi Ouzou, Tlemcen

**Highest Point**     Tahat 9,852 feet (3,003 m)

**Border Countries**     Libya, Mali, Mauritania, Morocco, Niger, Tunisia

**Official Language**     Arabic

**State Religion**     Islam

**Important holidays**     Eid al-Kebir, Eid al-Seghir, Historical Readjustment Day, Independence Day, Labour Day, New Year's Day, Revolution Day

**Population**     31,800,000 (2004 estimate)

**Natural Resources**     Iron ore, lead, natural gas, petroleum, phosphates, uranium, zinc

**Main Imports**     Consumer goods, foodstuffs

**Main Exports**     Natural gas, petroleum, petroleum products

**Industries**     Food processing, light industries, mining, natural gas, petrochemical, petroluem

**Agricultural Products**     Barley, citrus fruits, grapes, oats, olives, wheat

**Currency**     Algerian dinar (71.48 DZD = U.S. $1 as of 2004)

*Opposite:* **At a young age, Algerian children learn Arabic, the country's official language.**

# Glossary

## Arabic Vocabulary

*burek* (BOO-rek): egg, meat, and onion mixture in phyllo pastry.

*chaabi* (CHA-bee): Algerian folk music sung in Arabic.

*cheb* (SHABB): a male rai singer.

*cheikhs* (SHAKES): male singers of malhun.

*cheikhas* (SHAKE-has): women who entertained people in taverns with songs and dances.

*chorba* (CHOR-ba): a spicy stew of herbs, vegetables, and lamb or chicken.

*gourbi* (GUR-bee): a hut made of stone and brick.

*malhun* (mal-HOON): an Algerian style of sung poetry.

*moussem* (MOO-sem): local festivals.

*rai* (RYE): a style of Algerian popular music.

*ra'y* (RAH-ee): advice or opinion.

*shakshuka* (shak-SHOO-ka): a stew made with vegetables.

*tajine* (tah-JEEN): a stew made with lamb or chicken.

*wali* (WAH-lee): governor.

*wilayat* (wee-LIE-yat): provinces.

*wahrani* (wah-RAN-i): a variation of rai music.

## French Vocabulary

*colons* (KO-lens): colonists who settled in Algeria during French colonial rule.

*lycée* (lee-SAY): the French equivalent of high school.

## English Vocabulary

**alienation:** the state of feeling like an outcast.

**anti-Semitic:** characterized by hostility toward Jews on religious, ethnic, or racial grounds.

**apprenticed:** learned about a trade through practical experience.

**archaeologists:** scientists who study human life and activities by examining the fossil record, ruings, and artifacts of early peoples.

**baptistry:** the part of a church used for baptisms.

**basilica:** a building used as a court of justice and place of public assembly.

**cease-fire:** an order to end ongoing hostile activities, especially military actions.

**citadel:** a fortress that overlooks and controls a city.

**collaborated:** worked together with.

**coup d'etat:** sudden, often violent, political takeover by a small group.

**devout:** devoted to a belief.

**deys:** rulers of the Ottoman Empire in North Africa.

**dilapidated:** run down; partially ruined.

**disbanded:** broken up.

**disruptive:** causing chaos or disorder.

**distinctive:** standing out from a larger group.

**diversify:** to produce variety in.

**Eid al-Kebir:** the Muslim festival that celebrates Abraham's faith and devotion to God. Also called Eid al-Adha.

**Eid al-Seghir:** the Muslim festival that marks the end of Ramadan. Also called Eid al-Fitr.

**emancipation:** the freeing of a person or group from another's control.

**engravings:** pictures cut into a surface.

**extremists:** people who support extreme

**feminism:** the view that women have the same rights as men.

**flourishing:** growing; thriving.

**forums:** public meeting places for open discussion and audience participation

**fortified:** strengthened and secured.

**fraudulent:** deceitful.

**futility:** the quality of being useless.

**guerrilla tactics:** aggressive and unconventional military tactics, often meant to harrass or sabotage.

**hierarchical:** arranged according to rank or importance.

**hinterland:** a region inland from a coast.

**hydrocarbons:** compounds containing hydrogen and carbon; two such compounds are oil and natural gas.

**influential:** having influence or power.

**illiterate:** unable to read or write.

**kebobs:** cubes of marinated meat and vegetables on a skewer.

**laureate:** the recipient of an honor or achievement in art or science.

**literate:** able to read and write.

**marginalized:** treated as if unimportant.

**matrilineal:** having to do with the mother's side of the family.

**medina:** a non-European section of a city in North Africa.

**Moorish:** having to do with the Arabs that conquered Spain.

**nationalist groups:** groups that seek independence for a nation.

**ousted:** removed by force.

**outposts:** frontier settlements or bases.

**percussion:** having to do wtih the family of musical instruments that are struck to produce sound.

**phyllo pastry:** a flaky, layered pastry.

**plundered:** looted; took items by force.

**prestigious:** important in the eyes of others.

**prolific:** very productive.

**prominently:** greatly; known to many.

**Ramadan:** the Islamic period of compulsory fasting.

**referendum:** a mass vote in which the voters decide whether or not to adopt laws or policies.

**refrain:** to stop from doing something.

**retaliate:** take revenge.

**rhetoric:** the art of speaking or writing effectively.

**self-sufficient:** able to maintain itself without aid from others.

**semolina:** a grainy powder made from durum wheat.

**skirmishes:** minor battles between opposing parties, usually in a larger war.

**socialist:** having a system where the government controls and handles the distribution of all the goods and services within the society.

**suppressed:** put down by force.

**unleavened bread:** bread made without yeast.

**vassals:** people who are given land and protected by overlords in exchange for labor or service.

# More Books to Read

*A Traveller's History of North Africa*. *The Traveller's History* series. Barnaby Rogerson (Interlink Pub Group)

*Algeria*. *Cultures of the World* series. Falaq Kagda (Benchmark Books)

*Algeria in Pictures*. *Visual Geography* series. Lerner Geography Department, editor (Lerner Publishing Group)

*Mysteries of the Sahara: Chronicles from National Geographic*. *Culture and Geographical Exploration* series. Arthur Meier Schlesinger, editor (Chelsea House)

*The Middle East and North Africa*. *Regional Studies* series. Reeva S. Simon, editor (Globe Fearon)

*Sahara Unveiled: A Journey Across the Desert*. William Langewiesche (Vintage)

*Tuaregs*. Ann Carey Sabbah (Smart Apple Media)

# Videos

*Algeria's Bloody Years* (First Run/Icarus Films)

*Algeria: Women at War* (Formation Films)

*Arab Diaries: Love and Marriage* (First Run/Icarus Films)

*Battle of Algiers* (Rhino Video)

# Web Sites

inic.utexas.edu/menic/rai

lcweb2.loc.gov/frd/cs/dztoc.html

www.cia.gov/cia/publications/factbook/geos/ag.html

www.oxfam.org.uk/coolplanet/ontheline/explore/journey/algeria/alindex.htm

www.state.gov/r/pa/ei/bgn/8005.htm

Due to the dynamic nature of the Internet, some web sites stay current longer than others. To find additional web sites, use a reliable search engine with one or more of the following keywords to help you locate information about Algeria. Keywords: *Algiers, Berbers, Constantine, Ghardaïa, Kasbah, rai, Sahara Desert, Tassili n'Ajjer, Tuaregs.*

# Index